Also by Edward Eager

HALF MAGIC

EDWARD EAGER

ILLUSTRATED BY
N. M. BODECKER

HOUGHTON MIFFLIN HARCOURT

Boston   New York

hmhbooks.com

Hand lettering by Maeve Norton

The Library of Congress has cataloged the hardcover edition as follows:
Eager, Edward.
Half magic/Edward Eager; illustrated by N. M. Bodecker.
p. cm.
Sequel: Magic by the lake.
Summary: Faced with a dull summer in the city, Jane, Mark,
Katharine, and Martha suddenly find themselves involved in a
series of extraordinary adventures after Jane discovers an
ordinary-looking coin that seems to grant wishes.
[1. Magic—Fiction. 2. Wishes—Fiction. 3. Space and time—Fiction.]
I. Bodecker, N. M., ill. II. Title.
PZ7.E115Hal 1999
[Fic]—dc21 99-24558

ISBN: 978-0-544-67172-0 paperback

Printed in the United States of America
DOC 10
4500798004

Contents

The Magician of *Half Magic*

BY ALICE HOFFMAN

I've always believed that the books that influence us most are the ones we read at the age of ten or eleven or twelve, the time when we're most open to imagination and magic, when the world hasn't yet made us the rational and boring beings most adults grow up to be. If you're lucky, you will be exactly this age when you discover a writer who teaches you about the world, and about literature, and, for those who are the luckiest of all, about magic.

Of course the best magic is when extraordinary things happen to ordinary people, unexpectedly and out of the blue. This is the way magic begins in folktales and fairy tales: Once upon a time, on a day like any other, a boy like you, or a girl like me, found a charm or a beast or a book that changed everything, allowing us to see beyond our own lives, into the realm of possibilities.

I found the book that changed my life one summer day, stocked on a dusty shelf at the library. I'd never heard of the author, but when I saw the title I knew it was exactly what I'd been looking for. After the first few pages, I was utterly hooked. I read Edward Eager all that summer while school was out, and I highly recommend my child-reader friends do the same. Make one summer your Edward Eager summer and you will never forget it. Other summers will become hazy and forgettable, but for this one summer everything you do will be touched by magic. Edward Eager once wrote: "The next best thing to having it actually happen to you is to read about it." Readers know this is absolutely true. I read *Half Magic* and my life was never the same. The door to my imagination was unlocked, and every time I walked to the library, every time I made a wish, every time I started to read a book, I knew magic was a distinct possibility.

* * *

Edward Eager, born 1911, was a lyricist and dramatist. He was a witty, sophisticated writer from Connecticut who stumbled into the realm of children's books after discovering the work of the English author E. Nesbit in 1947 while searching for novels to read to his beloved son, Fritz. For Eager, what made Nesbit great was the way she managed to integrate magic into real life. "For if there is one thing that makes E. Nesbit's magic books more enchanting than any others, it is not that they are funny, or exciting, or beautifully written, or full of wonderfully alive and endearing children, all of which they are." It was "the *dailiness* of the magic" that appealed to Edward Eager. "So after you finish reading one of her stories you feel it could all happen to *you,* any day now, round any corner." The same can be said of all of Eager's wonderful books, all filled with the power of the imagination and the possibility that anything can happen at any time, to anyone. As a plus, Eager's style is funny, wise, and entertaining. He loves jokes and puns and has real empathy for characters who are human, sometimes to a fault, but who learn from their mistakes.

With his first book, *Half Magic,* Eager succeeded in writing a work of genius, a classic story about magic and daily life and, as in all of his novels, about the love of books. *Half Magic* begins the series of seven Tales of Magic that Eager would go on to write before his untimely death at the age of fifty-three. But as we all know, seven is the most magical of numbers, and the first book is always the best. The fun begins with a talisman found on the sidewalk on the way home from a visit to the library. Magic, Eager believed, is unpredictable and unreliable; it has to be understood and tamed, which is half the fun and delight of *Half Magic*. "Always remember that magic has a mind of its own and will thwart you if it can," Eager wrote. The mischief-making talisman the children discover grants only half-wishes, although this takes a while to grasp. They must figure out how to properly use the powerful and ancient charm, and many mistakes are made, with adventures had and lessons learned.

In *Half Magic,* as in all of Eager's Tales of Magic, children see what adults cannot. They haven't yet lost the ability to appreciate what is wondrous in the world. But even children have to rethink their practical lives and acknowledge that magic is a possibility. The children in *Half Magic* are convinced that magic could never happen to them — until what looks like an old nickel turns out to be the charm that changes their lives. Soon enough they discover the power of a wish, and how easily a wish can go wrong if you don't consider the consequences. The world of magic is a puzzle, much like the rest of life, and by the time the children have figured out the rules, they must move on into the next phase, and give the magic over to the next child who needs to have his or her own adventures.

A real writer remembers what it is like to be a reader, and a great children's book writer remembers what it was like to be a child. "There are lucky people who never lose the gift of seeing the world as a child sees it, a magic place where anything can happen next minute, and delightful and unexpected things constantly do." Edward Eager was one of these people. And *Half Magic* is one of the books you never forget.

Jane was the oldest, Mark was the only boy, Katherine was the middle girl, and Martha was the youngest and "very difficult." These four children find great joy in walking two miles to the library, as I did in the summer. Eager wrote the book in the 1950s, and the time period of *Half Magic* is the 1920s—yet the book feels timeless and the children could easily be our next-door neighbors.

The sorrow that hangs over these ordinary children is that their father has died and they worry for their mother's happiness and for the fate of their family. They happen to meet Mr. Smith, who they soon discover would make an excellent stepfather, for unlike most adults he advocates believing six impossible things before breakfast. Once the children figure out the magic's formula (having started a half-fire, brought a group of friends half-home, and have their cat wonderfully half-talk), they learn to double their wishes and travel to the desert and to Camelot; then, headstrong Jane wishes she belonged to another family (as many of us have wished at one time or another) only to regret it and to realize, along with her brother and sisters and mother, that magic is no longer necessary. They already have their hearts' desire: each other.

My own writing, both for children and adults, has been hugely influenced by Edward Eager and his brand of suburban magic, or what I call practical magic. When there are no enchanted woods or fairy-tale castles and only a small town where magic seems unlikely, anything can happen if you know where to look. Often the best place to discover magic is in a book, on a summer day, on the walk home from the library. Begin by reading *Half Magic* and the enchantment will already be halfway there.

Alice Hoffman is the author of many books for children, including *Aquamarine*, *Green Angel*, and *Nightbird*. Her books for adults include *Practical Magic*, *The Museum of Extraordinary Things*, *The Dovekeepers*, and *The Marriage of Opposites*. *Half Magic* is her favorite book for children and Edward Eager is her favorite children's book author.

1

How It Began

It began one day in summer about thirty years ago, and it happened to four children.

Jane was the oldest and Mark was the only boy, and between them they ran everything.

Katharine was the middle girl, of docile disposition and a comfort to her mother. She knew she was a comfort, and docile, because she'd heard her mother say so. And the others knew she was, too, by now, because ever since that day Katharine *would* keep boasting about what a comfort she was, and how docile, until Jane declared she would utter a piercing shriek and fall over dead if she heard another word about it. This will give you some idea of what Jane and Katharine were like.

Martha was the youngest, and very difficult.

The children never went to the country or a lake in the summer, the way their friends did, because their father was dead and their mother worked very hard on the other newspaper, the one almost nobody on the block took. A woman named Miss Bick came in every day to care for the children, but she couldn't seem to care for them very much, nor they for her. And she wouldn't take them to the country or a lake; she said it was too much to expect and the sound of waves affected her heart.

"Clear Lake isn't the ocean; you can hardly hear it," Jane told her.

"It would attract lightning," Miss Bick said, which Jane thought cowardly, besides being unfair arguing. If you're going to argue, and Jane usually was, you want people to line up all their objections at a time; then you can knock them all down at once. But Miss Bick was always sly.

Still, even without the country or a lake, the summer was a fine thing, particularly when you were at the beginning of it, looking ahead into it. There

would be months of beautifully long, empty days, and each other to play with, and the books from the library.

In the summer you could take out ten books at a time, instead of three, and keep them a month, instead of two weeks. Of course you could take only four of the fiction books, which were the best, but Jane liked plays and they were nonfiction, and

Katharine liked poetry and that was nonfiction, and Martha was still the age for picture books, and they didn't count as fiction but were often nearly as good.

Mark hadn't found out yet what kind of nonfiction he liked, but he was still trying. Each month he would carry home his ten books and read the four good fiction ones in the first four days, and then read one page each from the other six, and then give up. Next month he would take them back and try again. The nonfiction books he tried were mostly called things like "When I was a Boy in Greece," or "Happy Days on the Prairie"—things that made them sound like stories, only they weren't. They made Mark furious.

"It's being made to learn things not on purpose. It's unfair," he said. "It's sly." Unfairness and slyness the four children hated above all.

The library was two miles away, and walking there with a lot of heavy, already-read books was dull, but coming home was splendid—walking slowly, stopping from time to time on different strange front steps, dipping into the different books. One day Katharine, the poetry-lover, tried to read *Evangeline* out loud on the way home, and Martha sat right down on the sidewalk after seven blocks of it, and refused to go a step farther if she had to hear another word of it. That will tell you about Martha.

After that Jane and Mark made a rule that nobody could read bits out loud and bother the others. But this summer the rule was changed. This summer the children had found some books by a writer named E. Nesbit, surely the most wonderful books in the world. They read every one that the library had, right away, except a book called *The Enchanted Castle,* which had been out.

And now yesterday *The Enchanted Castle* had come in, and they took it out, and Jane, because she could read fastest and loudest, read it out loud all the way home, and when they got home she went on reading, and when their mother came home they hardly said a word to her, and when dinner was served they didn't notice a thing they ate. Bedtime came at the moment when the magic ring in the book changed from a ring of invisibility to a wishing ring. It was a terrible place to stop, but their mother had one of her strict moments; so stop they did.

And so naturally they all woke up even earlier than usual this morning, and Jane started right in reading out loud and didn't stop till she got to the end of the last page.

There was a contented silence when she closed the book, and then, after a little, it began to get discontented.

Martha broke it, saying what they were all thinking.

"Why don't things like that ever happen to *us?*"

"Magic never happens, not really," said Mark, who was old enough to be sure about this.

"How do you know?" asked Katharine, who was nearly as old as Mark, but not nearly so sure about anything.

"Only in fairy stories."

"It *wasn't* a fairy story. There weren't any dragons or witches or poor woodcutters, just real children like us!"

They were all talking at once now.

"They *aren't* like us. We're never in the country for the summer, and walk down strange roads and find castles!"

"We never go to the seashore and meet mermaids and sand fairies!"

"Or go to our uncle's, and there's a magic garden!"

"If the Nesbit children do stay in the city it's London, and *that's* interesting, and then they find phoenixes and magic carpets! Nothing like that ever happens here!"

"There's Mrs. Hudson's house," Jane said. "That's a *little* like a castle."

"There's the Miss Kings' garden."

"We could *pretend* . . ."

It was Martha who said this, and the others turned on her.

"Beast!"

"Spoilsport!"

Because of course the only way pretending is any good is if you never say right out that that's what you're doing. Martha knew this perfectly well, but in her youth she sometimes forgot. So now Mark threw a pillow at her, and so did Jane and Katharine, and in the excitement that followed their mother woke up, and Miss Bick arrived and started giving orders, and "all was flotsam and jetsam," in the poetic words of Katharine.

Two hours later, with breakfast eaten, Mother gone to work and the dishes done, the four children escaped at last, and came out into the sun. It was fine weather, warm and blue-skied and full of possibilities, and the day began well, with a glint of something metal in a crack in the sidewalk.

"Dibs on the nickel," Jane said, and scooped it into her pocket with the rest of her allowance, still jingling there unspent. She would get round to thinking about spending it after the adventures of the morning.

The adventures of the morning began with promise. Mrs. Hudson's house looked *quite* like an Enchanted Castle, with its stone wall around and iron dog on the lawn. But when Mark crawled into the peony bed and Jane stood on his shoulders and held Martha up to the kitchen window, all Martha saw was Mrs. Hudson mixing something in a bowl.

"Eye of newt and toe of frog, probably," Katharine thought, but Martha said it looked more like simple one-egg cake.

And then when one of the black ants that live in all peony beds bit Mark, and he dropped Jane and Martha with a crash, nothing happened except Mrs. Hudson's coming out and chasing them with a broom the way she always did, and saying she'd tell their mother. This didn't worry them much, because their mother always said it was Mrs. Hudson's own fault, that people who had trouble with children brought it on themselves, but it was boring.

So then the children went farther down the street and looked at the Miss Kings' garden. Bees were humming pleasantly round the columbines, and there were Canterbury bells and purple foxgloves looking satisfactorily old-fashioned, and for a moment it seemed as though anything might happen.

But then Miss Mamie King came out and told them that a dear little fairy lived in the biggest purple foxglove, and this wasn't the kind of talk the children wanted to hear at all. They stayed only long enough to be polite, before trooping dispiritedly back to sit on their own front steps.

They sat there and couldn't think of anything exciting to do, and nothing went on happening, and it was then that Jane was so disgusted that she said right out loud she wished there'd be a fire!

The other three looked shocked at hearing such wickedness, and then they looked more shocked at what they heard next.

What they heard next was a fire siren!

Fire trucks started tearing past—the engine, puffing out smoke the way it used to do in those days, the Chief's car, the hook and ladder, the chemicals!

Mark and Katharine and Martha looked at Jane,

and Jane looked back at them with wild wonder in her eyes. Then they started running.

The fire was eight blocks away, and it took them a long time to get there, because Martha wasn't allowed to cross streets by herself, and couldn't run fast yet, like the others; so, they had to keep waiting for her to catch up, at all the corners.

And when they finally reached the house where the trucks had stopped, it wasn't the house that was on fire. It was a playhouse in the backyard, the fanciest playhouse the children had ever seen, two stories high and with dormer windows.

You all know what watching a fire is like, the glory of the flames streaming out through the windows, and the wonderful moment when the roof falls in, or even better if there's a tower and it falls through the roof. This playhouse *did* have a tower, and it fell through the roof most beautifully, with a crash and a shower of sparks.

And the fact that it *was* a playhouse, and small like the children, made it seem even more like a special fire that was planned just for them. And the little girl the playhouse belonged to turned out to be an unmistakably spoiled and unpleasant type named

Genevieve, with long golden curls that had probably never been cut; so *that* was all right. And furthermore, the children overheard her father say he'd buy her a new playhouse with the insurance money.

So altogether there was no reason for any but feelings of the deepest satisfaction in the breasts of the four children, as they stood breathing heavily and watching the firemen deal with the flames, which they did with that heroic calm typical of fire departments the world over.

And it wasn't until the last flame was drowned, and the playhouse stood there a wet and smoking mess of ashes and charred boards, that guilt rose up in Jane and turned her joy to ashes, too.

"Oh, what you did," Martha whispered at her.

"I don't want to talk about it," Jane said. But she went over to a woman who seemed to be the nurse of the golden-haired Genevieve, and asked her how it started.

"All of a piece it went up, like the Fourth of July as ever was," said the nurse. "And it's my opinion," she added, looking at Jane very suspiciously, "that it was *set!* What are *you* doing here, little girl?"

Jane turned right around and walked out of the

yard, holding herself as straight as possible and trying to keep from running. The other three went after her.

"Is Jane magic?" Martha whispered to Katharine.

"I don't know. I think so," Katharine whispered back.

Jane glared at them. They went for two blocks in silence.

"Are we magic, too?"

"I don't know. I'm scared to find out."

Jane glared. Once more silence fell.

But this time Martha couldn't hold herself in for more than half a block.

"Will we be burnt as *witches?*"

Jane whirled on them furiously.

"I wish," she started to say.

"Don't!" Katharine almost screamed, and Jane turned white, shut her lips tight, and started walking faster.

Mark made the others run to catch up.

"This won't do any good. We've got to talk it over," he told Jane.

"Yes, talk it over," said Martha, looking less worried. She had great respect for Mark, who was a boy and knew everything.

"The thing is," Mark went on, "was it just an accident, or did we want so much to be magic we *got* that way, somehow? The thing is, each of us ought to make a wish. That'll prove it one way or the other."

But Martha balked at this. You could never tell with Martha. Sometimes she would act just as grown-up as the others, and then suddenly she would be a baby. Now she was a baby. Her lip trembled, and she said she didn't want to make a wish and she *wouldn't* make a wish and she wished they'd never started to play this game in the first place.

After consultation, Mark and Katharine decided this could count as Martha's wish, but it didn't seem to have come true, because if it had they wouldn't remember any of the morning, and yet they remembered it all too clearly. But just as a test Mark turned to Jane.

"What have we been doing?" he asked.

"Watching a fire," Jane said bitterly, and at that moment the fire trucks went by on their way home to the station, to prove it.

So then Mark rather depressedly wished his shoes were seven-league boots, but when he tried to jump seven leagues it turned out they weren't.

Katharine wished Shakespeare would come up

and talk to her. She forgot to say exactly *when* she wanted this to happen, but after they waited a minute and he didn't appear, they decided he probably wasn't coming.

So it seemed that if there was any magic among them, Jane had it all.

But try as they might, they couldn't persuade Jane to make another wish, even a little safe one. She just kept shaking her head at all their arguments, and when argument descended to insult she didn't say a word, which was most unlike Jane.

When they got home she said she had a headache, and went out on the sleeping porch, and shut the door. She wouldn't even come downstairs for lunch, but stayed out there alone all the afternoon, moodily eating a whole box of Social Tea biscuits and talking to Carrie, the cat. Miss Bick despaired of her.

When their mother came home she knew something was wrong. But being an understanding parent, she didn't ask questions.

At dinner she announced that she was going out for the evening. Jane didn't look up from her brooding silence, but the others were interested. The children always hoped their mother was going on exciting adventures, though she seldom was. Tonight she was going to see Aunt Grace and Uncle Edwin.

"Why?" Mark wanted to know.

"They were very kind to me after your father died. They have been very kind to you."

"Useful presents!" Mark was scornful.

"Will Aunt Grace say 'Just a little chocolate cake, best you ever tasted, I made it myself?'" Katharine wanted to know.

"You shouldn't laugh at your Aunt Grace. I don't know what your father would say."

"Father laughed at her, too."

"It isn't the same thing."

"Why?"

This kind of conversation was always very interesting to the children, and could have gone on forever so far as they were concerned, but somehow no grown-ups ever seemed to feel that way about conversations. Their mother put a stop to this one by leaving for Aunt Grace's.

When she had gone, things got strange again. Jane kept hovering in and out of the room where the others were playing a halfhearted game of Flinch, until everyone was driven wild.

Finally Mark burst out.

"Why don't you tell us?"

Jane shook her head.

"I can't. You wouldn't understand."

Naturally this made everyone furious.

"Just because she's magic she thinks she's smarter!" Martha said.

"*I* don't think she's magic at all!" This was Katharine. "Only she's afraid to make a wish and find out!"

"I'm not! I *am!*" Jane cried, not very clearly. "Only I don't know why, or how much! It's like having one foot almost asleep, but not quite—you can't use it and you can't enjoy it! I'm afraid to even *think* a wish! I'm afraid to think at *all!*"

If you have ever had magic powers descend on you suddenly out of the blue, you'll know how Jane felt.

When you have magic powers and know it, it can be a fine feeling, like a pleasant tingling inside. But in order to enjoy that tingling, you have to know just how much magic you have and what the rules are for using it. And Jane didn't have any idea how much she had or how to use it, and this made her unhappy and the others couldn't see why, and said so, and Jane answered back, and by the time they went to bed no one was speaking to anyone else.

What bothered Jane most was a feeling that she'd forgotten something, and that if she could remember it she'd know the reason for everything that had happened. It was as if the reason were there in her mind somewhere, if only she could reach it. She leaned into her mind, reaching, reaching . . .

The next thing she knew, she was sitting straight up in bed and the clock was striking eleven, and she had remembered. It was as though she'd gone on thinking in her sleep. Sometimes this happens.

She got up and felt her way to the dresser where she'd put her money, without looking at it, when she came home from the fire. First she felt the top of the dresser. Then she lit the lamp and looked.

The nickel she'd found in the crack in the sidewalk was gone.

And then Jane began thinking really hard.

2

What Happened to Their Mother

At Aunt Grace and Uncle Edwin's the air was hot and stuffy and the furniture was hot and stuffy and Aunt Grace and Uncle Edwin were stuffy.

"Poor things, they're so kind, really," the children's mother thought to herself.

But she had to remind herself of this very hard when Aunt Grace got out the snapshot albums.

"Now I know you'll be interested in these pictures of our trip to Yellowstone Park, Alison." Aunt Grace settled herself among the cushions of the davenport as though she expected to stay there a long time.

"I think you showed them to me last time, Aunt Grace."

"No, no, dear, that was *Glacier* Park. Edwin, move the floor lamp so Alison can see. This is the Old Faithful geyser. It comes up faithfully every hour, you see. That woman standing there isn't anyone we know. It's some woman from Ohio who kept trying to get in the picture. Edwin had to speak to her. Turn over the page."

The next page of the snapshot album showed Old Faithful from a different angle. The woman from Ohio had got only halfway into the picture; otherwise it looked just the same as the first one.

The children's mother patted back a yawn.

"I really must be going, Aunt Grace."

"Nonsense, dear. You must stay for cake and coffee. Just a little chocolate cake, best you ever tasted, I made it myself."

The children's mother suppressed a smile. Katharine had said Aunt Grace would say that—she always did.

The clock struck eleven.

"Oh, dear," their mother said to herself. "And

19

that long bus ride home, too! I wish I were home right now!"

Next moment all the lights in the room seemed to have gone out, only there seemed to be a moon and some stars shining in through the roof.

Their mother looked for Aunt Grace's stuffy, kind face, but Aunt Grace wasn't there. Instead, a clump of rather gangling milkweeds stared back at her. The hot, stuffy chair seemed suddenly to have grown cold and prickly. She looked down and around.

She was sitting on a weedy hummock by the side of a road. There were no houses in sight, nor any light but the far-off moon and stars.

What had happened? Had she suddenly gone mad? Or could she have said good-bye to Aunt Grace and Uncle Edwin, started to walk home instead of taking the bus, and then fainted?

But why couldn't she remember saying good-bye? Such a thing had never happened to her before in her life!

She thought she recognized the stretch of road before her. Aunt Grace and Uncle Edwin lived in a suburb, with half a mile of open country between them and the town. Half a mile with only one bus stop, the children's mother remembered. She must be somewhere in that half-mile, but would the bus stop be ahead or behind her?

The sky ahead showed a glow from the lights of town, and she started walking toward it.

The moon was a thin new one and didn't shed much light, and the woodsy thickets on either side of the road were dark and spooky. Things moved in the branches of trees. The children's mother didn't like it at all.

What was she, a successful newspaperwoman and the mother of four children, doing, wandering the roads by night like this?

When she was set upon and murdered by highwaymen and her body was found next morning, what would the children think? What would anyone think? It must be a bad dream. Soon she would wake up. Now she would keep walking.

She kept walking.

Behind her an engine throbbed and lights shone. She turned, holding up her hand, hoping it was the bus.

It wasn't the bus, just someone's car. But the car stopped by her, and rather a small gentleman looked out.

"Would you like a ride?"

"Well, no, not really," the children's mother said, which was not true at all; she would like one very much. But she had always told the children particularly not to go riding with strangers.

"Did your car break down?"

"Well, no, not exactly."

"Just taking a walk?"

"Well, no."

The rather small gentleman had opened the door of the car now.

"Get in," he said.

To her surprise, the children's mother got in. They rode along for a bit in silence. The children's mother tried to study the gentleman's face out of the corner of her eye, and was displeased to see that he wore a beard. Beards always seemed to her rather sinister. Why would anyone wear one, unless he had something to hide?

But this beard was only a small, pointed one, and the rest of the gentleman's face, or as much of it as she could see in the dark car, seemed pleasant. She found herself wanting to tell him of her strange adventure. Of course she couldn't. It would sound too silly.

The gentleman broke the silence.

"Lonely out this way after dark," he said. "Rather dangerous for walking, I should say."

"I should say so, too," said the children's mother. "I can't think what can have happened. There I was, talking to Aunt Grace, and suddenly *there* I was, by the side of the road!"

And, in spite of having decided not to, she began telling the small gentleman all about it.

"There's only one explanation," she said, at the end of it. "I must have lost my memory, just for a minute."

"Oh, there's never only *one* explanation," said the rather small gentleman. "It depends on which one you want to believe! I believe in believing six impossible things before breakfast, myself. Not that I usually get the chance. The trouble with life is that not enough impossible things happen for us to believe in, don't you agree? Where did you say you live?"

"I didn't," said the children's mother. Really, this night was growing odder and odder. She wasn't used to meeting people who talked exactly like the White Queen, or to giving her address to perfect strangers, either—still, if she wanted to get home there didn't seem to be anything else to do.

She gave him her address, and a moment later they were driving up before the house.

She thanked the small gentleman for his trouble. He bowed, hesitated as though he meant to say something further, then seemed to think better of it, and drove away.

It wasn't until he was gone that the children's mother realized that she didn't even know his name, nor he hers. Still, they would probably never see each other again.

She turned and started up the walk, then stopped in horror.

All the lights in the living room were ablaze!

Thinking of every terrible thing that could possibly have happened, she ran up the walk, turned her key in the lock, and hurried inside.

Huddled on a corner of the sofa sat Jane, wrapped in a blanket and looking small and white and forlorn.

Her mother was by her side and had her arms round her in a second. All thoughts of her own strange evening, and of the rather small gentleman, vanished from her head.

"What is it, tummy-ache or bad dreams?" she cried. "You should have telephoned me!"

"It isn't either one," Jane said. "Mother, did you borrow a nickel that was on my dresser?"

"*What?*" cried her mother. "Did you wait up all this time to ask me *that?*"

And immediately she began to scold, as is the habit of parents when they've been worried about their children and find that they needn't have been.

"Really, Jane, you must *not* be so money-grub-
bing!" she said. "Yes, I borrowed a nickel for carfare. I only had one nickel and a five-dollar bill, and
they're always so mean about making change . . ."

"Did you *spend* it?" Jane interrupted, her voice
horrified.

"I spent a nickel, going. What does it matter? I'll
pay you back tomorrow."

"Did you spend the other nickel, coming home?"

Her mother looked confused, for a moment.

"Well, no, as a matter of fact I didn't. Someone
gave me a lift."

"Do you know which one you spent, the one you
had or the one you borrowed?"

"Oh, for Heaven's sake! No, I don't!"

"Could I have the one you didn't spend? Now,
please?"

"Jane, what *is* all this? Anyone would think you
were a starving Little Match Girl, or something!"
Then her mother relented. "Oh well, if it'll make
you happy!"

She dug in her purse.

"Here. Now go to bed."

Jane took one quick look at the thing her mother

had given her, then folded her hand tightly around it. She had guessed right. It wasn't a nickel.

She lingered in the doorway.

"Mother."

"What is it now?"

"Well, did you . . . did anything . . . anything sort of *unusual* happen tonight?"

"What do you mean? Of course not! Why?"

"Oh, nothing!"

Jane searched in her mind for an excuse. She couldn't tell her mother the truth; she'd never believe it. It would only upset her.

"It's just that I . . . I had this *dream* about you, and I got worried. I dreamed you *wished* for something!"

"You did? That's strange." Her mother looked interested suddenly. She went on, almost to herself, as though she were remembering. "As a matter of fact, I *did* wish something. I wished I were at home. And it was just then that . . ."

"That *what?*" Jane was excited.

Her mother put on her "drop the subject" expression.

"Nothing. I came home. Someone gave me a ride. A . . . a friend of Uncle Edwin's."

27

She didn't look at Jane. It was awful to be lying like this, to her own child. But she couldn't tell Jane the truth; she'd never believe it. It would only upset her.

"I see." But Jane didn't leave. She stood tracing a pattern in the hall carpet with one foot. She went on carefully, not looking at her mother.

"In my dream, when you wished you were home, I'm not sure what came next. I don't think you *were* home, exactly . . ."

"Ha! I certainly wasn't!"

"But you were *somewhere!*"

"Somewhere in a weed patch, halfway out Bancroft Street, most likely!"

Now Jane looked up, and straight at her.

"We're just talking about my dream, aren't we? It didn't really happen?"

"Of course not."

It was her mother who was looking away now. But now Jane knew.

Clutching the thing in her hand tighter, she ran up the stairs and into her room.

Her mother stood thinking. How strange that Jane should have guessed! No stranger, though, than everything else about this strange evening. Probably none of it had really happened at all. Probably she was ill and imagining things—coming down with flu or something. She had better get some rest. She turned out the living room lights and went upstairs.

Jane stood in her own room, looking at the thing in her hand. It was the size of a nickel and the shape of a nickel and the color of a nickel, but it wasn't a nickel.

It was worn thin—probably by centuries of time, Jane told herself. And instead of a buffalo or a Liberty head, it bore strange signs. Jane held it closer to the light to study the signs.

There was a rap at the door.

"Lights out!" called her mother's voice.

Jane put out the light.

But she knew that she held in her hand the talisman that was going to turn this summer into a time of wild adventure and delight for all of them.

She must hide it in a safe place till morning.

Feeling her way across the room in the dark, she opened the closet door. There was a shoebag on the inside of the door, one of those flowered cotton affairs with many compartments for shoes, though Jane seldom remembered to put hers away in it.

She dropped the magic thing into one of the compartments in the shoebag. No one would disturb it there.

Then she got into bed.

Her last thought was that she must wake up early in the morning, by dawn at *least,* and call the others.

They must hold a Conference, and decide just how they were going to use this wonderful gift that had descended upon them out of the blue.

It was going to be an Enchanted Summer!

And Jane fell asleep.

3
What Happened to Mark

Of course it didn't work out that way at all.

In the morning Jane was so tired from her mid-night vigil that she slept right through breakfast. Their mother (who was tired, too) thought Jane needed the rest, and told Miss Bick not to call her.

Miss Bick looked disapproving as usual, but did as she was told. The children's mother went off to work, and Katharine and Martha (under protest) washed and dried the breakfast dishes without the usual charming companionship of their elder sister. Katharine was the washer and Martha the drier.

"I'd like to know what's going on around here," Katharine complained, over the cereal bowls. "Lights on at all hours and Mother and Jane holding secret midnight conspiracies in the living room. I heard them! And now Mother letting Jane stay in bed half the morning—I don't know what this house is coming to!"

"It's that magic. It's mysterious. I don't like it," Martha said.

Katharine had reached the awful pans that needed scouring now, and Martha went away and left her with them, as is the traitorous habit of all dish-driers.

She went into Jane's room. Drawn shades and a huddled form in the bed greeted her.

"Wake up," she said to the form, in a half-hearted way.

"Go away," said Jane, from under a sheet and blanket.

Martha felt depressed.

Carrie the cat had followed her into the room. Carrie's full name was Carrie Chapman Cat. Katharine had named her after a famous lady whose name she had seen in the newspaper. Carrie was a fat, not very interesting cat, kept mainly for mousing purposes, and the children ordinarily paid very little attention to her, or she to them.

But this morning everything was so gloomy and strange that Martha felt the need of comfort. She sat down on the floor, leaned her head back against the open door of Jane's closet, took Carrie in her lap, and stroked her.

There was a silence, except for the heavy breathing of Jane.

Martha felt a wish for companionship.

"Oh dear, if you could only talk," she said to Carrie.

"Purrxx," said Carrie the cat. "Wah oo merglitz. Fitzahhh!"

"What?" said Martha, startled.

"Wah oo merglitz," said Carrie. "Widl. Wifi uzz."

"Oh!" said Martha. "Oh!"

She got up, dropping Carrie rather heavily to the floor, and backed away, white with horror.

"Foo!" said Carrie resentfully. "Idgwit! At urt!"

Mark appeared in the doorway.

"Are my roller skates in here?" he demanded. "Jane borrowed them last week when her strap broke."

Martha ran to him and clutched him.

"It's that magic! *I've* got it now!" she cried. "I wished Carrie could talk, and now listen to her!"

Carrie chose this moment to put on an offended silence.

"Bushwah," Mark said gruffly. He had found his roller skates in Jane's shoebag and was putting them on. "That old cat. She always was crazy, anyway!"

"Azy ooselfitz!" said Carrie suddenly.

Mark looked surprised. Then he shook his head in disbelief.

"That's not talking," he said. "Probably just having a fit or something."

"But I wished she could talk, and then it began. Like Jane yesterday!"

"Just a coincidence," said Mark. "Yesterday, too. I don't believe in that old magic. Just Jane being smart. Just a lot of crazy girls."

He banged away through the house and out the front door, on his skates. Miss Bick could be heard, following in his wake and lamenting the fate of the floor polish.

Martha gave up. There was no sense in appealing to Mark in this mood. Sometimes he got tired of being the only boy in a family of girls, and when that happened there was no comfort in him. But she refused to be left here alone with the sleeping Jane and the gibbering Carrie.

Or could Mark have been right? Was it just a co-incidence? She looked at Carrie doubtfully.

"Did you say something?" she inquired politely.

"Idlwidl baxbix!" said Carrie. "Wah. Oom. Powitzer grompaw."

Martha fled the room, calling for Katharine.

Katharine met her in the hall.

"Don't talk to *me!*" she said. "Pan-shirker!"

"Oh, Kathie, don't be cross!" Martha entreated. "Something terrible's happened! *I've* got it now, only it comes all wrong!"

And she told Katharine of the behavior of Carrie.

The two sisters, clutched in each other's arms, cautiously approached the door of Jane's room and looked in.

Carrie was still there, pacing the floor, lashing her tail and muttering a horrid monologue.

"Idlwidl bixbax," she was saying. "Grompaw. Fooz! Idjwitz! Oo fitzwanna talkwitz inna fitzplace annahoo?"

She seemed to be trying desperately to express herself. It was agony to watch and still worse to hear.

"This can't go on," said Katharine.

She strode courageously into the room, making a wide circle around the still muttering Carrie, approached the huddled figure in the bed, and shook it.

"Fitzachoo!" said Jane.

"Now *she's* doing it!" Martha wailed, from the doorway.

Katharine looked shaken.

"I *think* it's just sleep-talk," she said. "The time has come for desperate measures."

"Let *me*," said Martha, glad to get away from the doorway even for a second.

She ran to the bathroom and fetched a wet sponge. Avoiding the sputtering Carrie, she ran back to the bed and trickled the sponge upon Jane.

Jane sat up in bed and struck her sister full in the face.

In the tears and apologies and mopping-up that followed, Jane awoke sufficiently to be engaged in sensible conversation and to notice the gurglings and spittings of Carrie.

"What did somebody do — wish she could talk?" she asked.

"Yes, *I* did. How did you know?" Martha stared in amazement.

"How did you happen to find the charm? Who told you you could go through my things?"

"I didn't! I don't know what you mean!"

"Wait a minute. Where were you standing when you wished it?"

"I wasn't. I was sitting down." And Martha showed her where.

"You must have leaned back and touched it."

"Touched *what?*" said Martha.

"*What* charm?" said Katharine.

"The charm in the shoebag," said Jane. "Wait till I tell you."

She told them.

"I don't see how you're so sure," said Martha, when she had finished. "About Mother last night, I mean."

"She just as good as said so," said Jane, "and I 'Sherlock Holmsed' the rest. Don't you see? She wished she were home and ended up *halfway* home! I wished there'd be a fire and got a *little* fire! A *child's-size* fire! Martha wished Carrie could talk and she can *half* talk!"

"Wah. Oom. Fitzbattleaxe," remarked Carrie.

"Exactly," said Jane. "It's that nickel I found, only it isn't a nickel! It's a magic charm and it does things by halves! So far we've each got *half* of what we wished for—all we have to do from now on is ask it for twice as much as we really want! You see?"

"I haven't had fractions yet," said Martha.

Jane explained further. Martha became weary of the explanation.

"What would twice as much as never having to learn fractions be?" she wanted to know, at last.

"Don't be silly—you don't want to ask it things like *that!*" Katharine cried in scorn.

"Nobody's going to ask for anything till we talk it over and decide," Jane announced firmly. "We don't want to waste any more wishes—we can't tell how soon we might wear it out! We'll make plans, and then take turns. My turn yesterday doesn't count, 'cause I didn't know. I get to go first, 'cause I'm the oldest."

"What would twice as much as not being the youngest anymore be?" was the bitter question of Martha, who was tired of always coming last.

But the others paid her no heed.

"*I* mean to ask for all kinds of really wonderful, exciting, important things!" Katharine was saying. "Only I'm not sure just what yet."

"Idjwitz! Selfitz! Fitz*me*fitz!" said Carrie, suddenly.

They looked at her in remorse. Now that they knew the reason for them, her outcries weren't so alarming anymore—they'd even almost forgotten about her. But, in spite of the fact that she seemed to be learning to express herself a little more clearly, she was plainly so enraged by her half-talking state that something had to be done.

"Poor Carrie, I'll fix you up first of all," Jane promised. "The charm's right in here."

She put her hand into the shoebag. But it wasn't.

She put her hand into another compartment. The charm wasn't there, either!

She began wildly searching through all the different sections, taking out pairs of shoes and shaking them. The magic thing wasn't in any of them. Jane began to get in one of her rages.

"Really, what a house!" she cried. "Nothing ever stays where you put it! Has Miss Bick been cleaning my room again?"

"No, she said it needed it but it was beyond her!"

"Mark!" was the next thought of Jane. "I *wondered* where he was! Has anyone seen him?"

"I did," reported Martha. "He came in here and got his roller skates, just a few minutes ago."

"*Roller skates!*" Jane's voice was a wail. "They were in the shoebag! He must have found the charm and taken it! A person might as well be living in a den of thieves around here!"

"I don't think he did," Martha said. "He said the whole thing was just a coincidence."

"He probably never noticed the magic charm at all," Katharine pointed out reasonably. "He probably just put the skates on with it *in* one of them, where you probably put it in the dark last night, without realizing. It probably got stuck down there in the tightening part. It's probably still there, only he probably doesn't know. He'll probably make a wish pretty soon, and then suddenly . . ."

"*Stop!*" Jane could bear no more. "We've got to find him! Before he wishes for some awful thing and gets half of it! Where do you suppose he could haven gone?"

Jane was rushing into her clothes now.

"Wah! *Mefitz! Mefitz!*" said Carrie, crossly.

"All right. We'll take you along." Martha, who was beginning to understand Carrie's half-language, hoisted her up under one arm.

They met Miss Bick in the hall.

"Where are you taking that cat?" she wanted to know.

"Idjwit! Foo! Fitzouta thewayfitz!" said Carrie savagely.

Miss Bick backed away, turning pale.

"That cat is *ill!*" she cried.

"I know. We're taking her to the vet's," Katharine called back over her shoulder.

Like everything else lately, the lie was only *half* an untruth. They *were* taking Carrie to be cured, if the charm could cure her.

The children emerged from the house, and stood looking around. Fortunately they lived on a corner lot, and could look down streets running in all four directions.

But no welcome sound of whirring skate wheels, no welcome sight of an eleven-year-old boy rewarded them. Finally they started hurrying south on Maplewood Avenue, not because south looked any more promising than east or north or west, but because they had to start somewhere. Martha tried to muffle the sounds Carrie kept making by holding her close to her, but the few passers-by they met kept turning to stare after them.

"Wah! Oom! Fitzpatrix!" Carrie screamed at the passers-by. She almost seemed to be enjoying herself.

"Hush. Hush," Martha told her. She was having hard work running fast enough to keep up with her sisters. "It won't be long now. At least, oh, I hope it won't!"

Meanwhile Mark had been skating around the neighborhood for some time. It was a dark, gloomy day and he wished the sun would come out. A minute later it did sort of half peep through the clouds.

Now that he was older, roller skating didn't seem quite the thing of whirlwind speed that it used to be, back in the days when it was new to him. He wished the skates would go faster. Pretty soon it seemed as though they did, a little.

But just skating around by himself wasn't very much fun. He wished all the guys were back from their vacations. He wished that when he came to the vacant lot up ahead, he'd see them there, playing baseball as usual.

And for a second, as he whizzed past the vacant lot, he did seem to sort of half-see a ghostly game in progress.

He rounded the corner and came down his own

block on Maplewood. As he passed Mrs. Hudson's house he wished, as he'd often wished before, that just for once the iron dog in the yard would be alive, instead of only iron.

Then he looked back. For a minute he thought he heard a faint muffled bark, and it seemed as though the iron tail had tried to wag. Mark guessed he must have a pretty vivid imagination, all right, the way Miss Amrhein, his last year's teacher, had always said.

Thinking of Miss Amrhein reminded him of school. Maybe somebody'd be hanging around the playground, somebody else who hadn't gone away for vacation. He turned at the corner, and skated down Monroe Street toward the school building.

It was just after Mark turned the corner that Jane and Katharine and Martha came out of the house and started hurrying down the street.

As they passed Mrs. Hudson's yard, Carrie the cat struggled out of Martha's arms and ran up to the iron dog.

"Yah!" she cried, hissing and spitting at him. "Fitzbully! Fitzmutt! Curfitz!"

A strangled growl came from within the iron dog,

and he strained forward, trembling, as though trying to lunge at Carrie.

Jane gave a cry of triumph.

"Look!" she cried. "It's half-alive! Mark must have been here! He must have wished! Hurry up—we're on the right track!"

Martha dragged Carrie away from the iron dog and rushed on after the others. At the corner they hesitated, then turned and ran down Monroe Street, toward the school.

Mark stood looking around the playground. It was deserted, as he might have known it would be. Disappointed, he hauled himself up on the trapeze bar, hung by his knees, and swung head downward. He almost—but not quite—wished it were time for school to begin again; so all the kids would be back. A person might as well be on a desert island as in this empty town!

The thought of desert islands reminded him that he hadn't reread *Robinson Crusoe* yet this year. He was still thinking about *Robinson Crusoe* when his sisters came running into the playground.

"Thank goodness we found you in time to warn you!" Jane cried. "What have you been doing?"

Mark, still hanging head downwards, looked up at her.

"I was just wishing we were all on a desert island," he said.

Next moment the trapeze seemed to give way and he fell heavily to the ground. But instead of landing on the scratchy gravel of the playground, he fell on hot sand.

He rolled over and looked around him. His sisters sat nearby, looking only a trifle less surprised than he felt. Above, a flaming-hot sun blazed in a cloudless sky. Otherwise there didn't seem to be anything anywhere but sand.

"What happened? Where are we?" he cried dazedly.

Jane sighed grimly.

"You just got half a wish," she told him. "Desert, yes. Island, no."

Mark looked around again. It was all too true. Desert there certainly was, but no welcome sight of distant waves graced the horizon—only more sand, mile on monotonous mile of it.

"It's all right," Jane went on, a bit wearily. "I just *do* wish everybody wouldn't keep wasting wishes, though! Take off your skates and I'll get us home again."

To make Mark understand even a part of the situation was the work of several moments. They told him about the half-fire, about Mother, about Carrie. At last he began to believe.

He took off one of the skates and shook it. Nothing happened. He took off the other skate and shook it.

Something metal shot through the air in a bright arc, glittering in the pitiless light of the desert sun, then fell into the sand.

Each of the children would have sworn that he knew just where the magic thing had fallen, and four pairs of hands set to work with a will, burrowing in the sandy hotness. One pair of paws set to work also, Carrie the cat having decided to be helpful for once. There was a good bit of getting in each other's way and arguing.

Five minutes later the magic charm had still not been found. The sand was beginning to feel hotter. Fingers were getting sorer and tempers shorter.

"Don't crawl where I'm digging," said Katharine to Martha.

"Don't dig where I'm crawling," said Martha to Katharine.

"The way that charm keeps not staying put," said Jane, "you'd think it *wanted* everything to work out wrong!"

Ten more minutes passed.

"I for one," said Martha, sitting back exhausted, "will never play in a sandbox again."

"All the perfumes of Arabia would not sweeten this old sand," agreed the poetical Katharine, also sitting back.

"But we have to find it!" Jane cried, still digging desperately. "Otherwise we'll never get home! We'll die of thirst and some Arab will find our bleached bones months later and never know who we were!"

"I'm thirsty now," said Martha. "I'm hungry, too," she added.

"How do we know this really *is* Arabia?" asked Mark. "Maybe it's just Death Valley."

"Either way," said Jane, "is small comfort. Keep digging. Though it *is* like looking for a camel in a needle's eye," she admitted.

It was then that the caravan appeared.

It was a rather shopworn-looking caravan, only three mangy camels with one ragged Arab driving them, and some very meager, empty-looking packs on the camels' backs, but it served to make plain to the four children that they were, in fact, in that fa-bled wasteland they had read of so much in fact and fiction.

"Lost in the Sahara!" cried Katharine dramati-cally.

Mark was more practical.

"Caravan ahoy!" he shouted. "S O S! Help! Lend a hand!"

The three mangy camels and the ragged Arab al-tered their course and came toward them.

As they drew nearer, the four children began to wish they wouldn't. The ragged Arab's expression was crafty, and definitely unattractive. As he came to a stop before them he smiled, which made him look more unpleasant than ever.

"Bismillah!" he said.

"How!" said Martha.

"What do you think he is, an Indian?" hissed Mark, under his breath. He addressed the Arab. "Allee samee show humble servant nearest oasis chop-chop?"

"He won't understand that either—that's Chinese!" said Jane.

But the Arab seemed to comprehend.

"Western children follow Achmed," he said.

Jane refused to go.

"We can't leave the charm!" she cried. "It's our only chance to get home!"

"We might get to a place where there's Western Union. We could cable Mother collect. She might send for us," said Katharine doubtfully.

"It would cost untold millions and take *ages!*" cried Jane. "I won't budge from this spot! We'll find the magic thing if we keep looking!"

But the Arab, Achmed, seized her by the arm and propelled her, none too gently, toward the nearest camel.

"Do what he says," Mark whispered to Jane. "We have to get some water, anyway. We can always find this spot again if we leave the roller skates to mark it."

He didn't add that his fear was that the wind might bury the skates in sand before they could return. He didn't mention some other fears that were bothering him, either.

Jane allowed the Arab to help her up onto the nearest camel. Mark helped Katharine climb onto the second one, and the Arab lifted Martha onto the third. With Mark and the Arab on foot, they started away over the desert.

After a bit, Jane began to enjoy the new sensation

of riding camel-back, and forgot the charm for the
moment. Katharine too seemed almost happy, but
the up-and-down motion made Martha seasick and
she begged to be taken down.

Mark helped her off the camel and she walked
along with him. But her short legs soon tired, and
her feet grew sore from the hot sand burning through

the thin soles of her shoes. Mark had to half-carry her and the going was slow. They lagged a bit behind the others.

What worried Mark was that he didn't trust Achmed the Arab. Achmed had been all too eager to take the children with him, and Mark didn't like his smile.

Presently Mark's fears were confirmed. Carrie

the cat seemed to be making friends with the third camel, the one Martha had been riding. She frisked along by the camel's side. The camel leaned his head down to hers. It almost looked as though they were conversing together, the way animals undoubtedly do.

A moment later Carrie ran back to Mark and Martha. Her fur was standing on end with anger and excitement.

"Foo! Idjwitz!" she hissed at Mark. "Fitzachmed fitzwicked! Fitzkidnap! Ransomowitz!"

"I was afraid of that," said Mark. "Who told you?"

"Fitzcamel!"

Martha began to cry.

"Don't worry," Mark told her. "We'll escape somehow."

But he wished he knew how. Fortunately just then the oasis came into sight, which distracted Martha's attention.

It wasn't a very big oasis—no Western Union—but there were two or three date palms and a spring of water. Everyone stopped for a welcome drink. The dates were delicious. Martha took off her shoes to cool her feet with water from the spring. There was a good deal of sand in her shoes, and as she shook it out it was Mark who first saw the round, shining, silvery thing that fell out with it.

Though he'd never had a real look at it before, he didn't need to be told what it was. His hand shot out and he caught the charm in mid-air before it could be lost again.

Katharine had seen it a second after Mark.

"I *told* you not to crawl where I was digging!" she told Martha.

Jane had seen it a second after Katharine.

"It's the charm!" she cried. "Wish us home! Here, let me!"

But the Arab, Achmed, was standing nearby, and had seen the shining thing, too. He strode forward, seized Mark by the wrist, and brought the silver charm close to his eyes, close enough to see the mystic marks on it.

The expression of his face changed. No longer did he look like a kidnapper who was planning and plotting wickedness. He looked like a righteous man who has caught a thief in his house, or even worse, in the temple of his gods. His voice was stern.

"Western child steal sacred charm," he cried. "Sacred charm lost many years. Give back!"

His hand closed on the charm but Mark's hand

53

had closed on it first. Mark said the only thing that came into his mind.

"I wish you were half a mile away!"

And immediately, of course, Achmed the Arab was *half* of half a mile, or a *quarter* of a mile, away. The children could just see him, like a tiny dot far off on the desert sands. But the dot was coming nearer, as Achmed ran toward them again.

"Quick! Let me—I'll get us home! You don't know how!" Jane cried to Mark, but Mark waved her away. He was thinking.

"After all, maybe the charm *did* belong to his race," he said.

"It belongs to us now!" said Jane.

"Losers weepers finders keepers!" said Katharine.

"But maybe it *was* stolen. From a temple or somewhere," said Mark, slowly. "You know how people used to be unjust to natives in the olden days. It doesn't seem fair."

The others had to agree that it didn't. All except Carrie, who was seldom troubled by noble motives.

"Fitzachmed fitzwicked!" she reminded Mark.

"After all, he *was* going to kidnap us!" agreed Martha.

"He *was?*" cried Jane and Katharine, in surprise and excitement.

"Yes, he was, but let's not go into that now," said Mark. "I'll tell you later. After all, maybe he wouldn't have if he weren't poor and downtrodden. And we're supposed to be kind to our enemies, aren't we?"

Achmed the Arab was coming nearer now. Mark waited till he was close enough for them to see his face. Then he spoke aloud a wish he had thought out very carefully.

"I wish that Achmed the Arab may have twice as much as he deserves of whatever it is that he would wish for with this charm!" Mark said.

And of course the charm, to which arithmetic was as nothing, cut the wish neatly in half and in that moment the Arab Achmed received as much as he deserved of happiness.

Suddenly there were five camels in the caravan instead of three. The camels were young and healthy instead of old and mangy. The harnesses were new and trim instead of old and worn through. The meager, empty-looking packs bulged with rich stuffs for trading.

A plump Arab lady appeared suddenly at Achmed's

side, leading six plump Arab children by the hand. She smiled coyly at Achmed.

Achmed stopped short and looked at the caravan, at the lady, at the Arab children. He gave a great cry of happiness. On his face a look of peace replaced the old crafty shiftiness. He turned toward the East and fell on his face on the sand. His voice lifted in what sounded like a prayer of thanksgiving.

And it was then that Mark, still waving away the proffered help of Jane, spoke aloud the second wish he had carefully thought out.

"I wish that the four of us, and Carrie the cat, may travel in the direction of home, only twice as far."

Next thing they knew, they were all sitting on their own front steps.

The first thing they did was walk down the street to Mrs. Hudson's house. The iron dog still trembled in half-life on the lawn.

At that moment Mrs. Hudson came out of the house, her market basket on her arm. She took one look at the shaking dog.

"Earthquake! Earthquake!" she cried, and ran back inside the house.

Mark, who was getting quite good at it, made a third wish.

"I wish that this dog," he said, "may be twice as alive or twice as un-alive as it wishes to be."

Immediately the dog stopped trembling and stood still and cold as iron (which it was again).

"Wouldn't you think it'd rather have been real?" said Katharine in wonder.

"I guess iron things are happier *being* iron," said Mark, who had learned a lot in one day.

The four children now turned to the case of Carrie the cat.

"Wouldn't you like to go on talking, only plainer?" asked Martha, who had grown to enjoy her conversations with her pet.

"Notonna fitztintype," said Carrie. "Fitzsilence fitzgolden!"

The others then decided that Mark had had enough wishes for one day and they would take on this problem.

"I wish that Carrie the cat couldn't talk any of the time!" said Martha, not stopping to think it out.

"Well, you certainly messed that up," said Carrie the cat. "Now of course I can't talk half the time but the rest of the time I can talk perfectly plainly, not that I want to, of course, but here I go, talk, talk, talk, and here I *will go* for the next thirty seconds, and then thirty seconds of silence I suppose, and then talk, talk, talk again, just as though I had anything to say, which I don't, being always one for quiet meditation myself; still, duty calls; so speak the words trippingly on the tongue, only three more seconds to go now, the rest is silence, Shakespeare!"

She broke off suddenly, but only for thirty seconds. Then she began again. The children held their ears till the next silent period. Then Katharine made a hurried suggestion.

"The thing is, we want her to just mew, the way she used to," she said. "The thing is to think of a word that has 'mew' for half of it."

"*I* know!" said Jane. And she made a wish. "I wish that Carrie the cat may in future say nothing but the word 'music.'"

"Sick!" said Carrie the cat. "Sick sick sick sick sick sick sick sick sick sick sick sick sick sick."

She *looked* sick.

"Better let me," said Mark. "I've had practice." He took the charm in his hand. "I wish that Carrie the cat may be exactly twice as silent as she wishes to be."

"Mew," said Carrie the cat. "Purr."

And without so much as a look of gratitude at

Mark for restoring her to normalcy, she hurried off after a passing robin.

Tired but happy, the children trooped homeward. It had been a long, full day, but everything had worked out beautifully in the end.

Miss Bick met them with reproaches for having stayed out all day and missed their lunch.

"Just wait till I tell your mother!" she said.

And the children did.

Their mother looked very grave that night, when Miss Bick had told her.

"I don't want you children wandering away from the house like that again," she said to them at dinner. "As a matter of fact, you may as well know — something rather frightening has been happening. There seems to be an epidemic of kidnapping, or at least lost children. We kept getting reports at the paper all day, from different lakes and camps and places. A lot of little boys have disappeared. Mostly friends of yours, Mark, I'm afraid. Freddy Fox and Richey Gould and Michael Robinson, only there's a report he turned up halfway home and doesn't know how he got there . . ."

Mark choked suddenly on his milk, and turned bright red.

He signaled the others in a private way the four children had. They finished dinner as soon as they could, and gathered in Mark's room.

"It's awful!" Mark cried, as soon as the door was safely shut. "I just remembered! This morning I wished all the guys were home. Now there they all are, halfway home and wandering the countryside! I've got to fix them up!"

He took the charm from his pocket, where he'd put it after the last wish of the afternoon.

"I wish all the guys I wished home to be back twice as far as they were before I wished!" he said.

The others agreed that that ought to do it. But Mark was still worried.

"We have to be careful from now on," he said. "We don't want any more mistakes. That could have been bad."

"We'll hide it in a safe place," said Jane, "until tomorrow."

"I know where," said Katharine.

She led the others to the room she shared with Martha. There was a loose board in the floor with a space under it that the children had used to hide things in, back in the days when they were young.

The children hid the charm in this secret place.

"A mouse might find it and make a wish," Martha objected.

But the others felt that half the wish of a mouse could do little to upset their plans.

They had many plans to make.

"We'll spend the night thinking up wishes," said Jane. "It'll be better from now on, because now we all *know*. We'll make sensible wishes from now on. Tomorrow the real fun will begin."

And, in a way, it did.

4

What Happened to Katharine

Next morning there were no secret meetings before breakfast.

Jane stayed in her room and Mark stayed in his room, and in the room they shared Katharine and Martha hardly conversed at all.

Each of the children was too busy making private plans and deciding on favorite wishes.

Breakfast was eaten in silence, but not without the exchange of some excited looks. The children's mother was aware that something was in the air, and wondered what new trial lay in store for her.

When their mother had gone to work and the dishes and other loathly tasks were done, the four children gathered in Katharine and Martha's room. Katharine had already checked to see that the charm still lay in its cubbyhole, unharmed by wish of mouse or termite.

Jane had drawn up some rules.

"The wishes are to go by turns," she said. "Nobody's to make any main wish that doesn't include all the rest of us. If there have to be any smaller wishes later on in the same adventure, the person who wished the main wish gets to make them, except in case of emergency. Like if he loses the charm and one of the other ones finds it. I get to go first."

Katharine had something to say about that.

"I don't see why," she said. "You always get dibs on first 'cause you're the oldest, and grown-ups always pick Martha 'cause she's the baby, and Mark has a wonderful double life with all this and being a boy, too! Middle ones never get any privileges at all! Besides, who hasn't had a wish of her own yet? Think back!"

It was true. Jane had had the half-fire, and Martha had made Carrie half-talk, and Mark had taken them to half of a desert island.

Jane had to agree that Katharine deserved a chance. But she couldn't keep from giving advice.

"We don't want any old visits with Henry Wadsworth Longfellow," she said. "Make it something that's fun for everybody."

"I'm going to," said Katharine. "But I can't decide between wishing we could all fly like birds and wishing we had all the money in the world."

"Those aren't any good," said Jane. "People always wish those in stories, and it never works out at *all!* They either fly too near the sun and get burned, or end up crushed under all the money!"

"We could make it *paper* money," suggested Katharine.

A discussion followed as to how many million dollars in large bills it would take to crush a person to death. By the time the four children got back to the subject of the magic charm, seventeen valuable minutes had been wasted.

But now Mark had an idea.

"We've found out the charm can take us through space," he said. "What about time?"

"You mean travel around in the past?" Jane's eyes were glowing. "See Captain Kidd and Nero?"

"I've always wanted to live back in the olden romantic days," said Katharine, getting excited, too. "In days of old when knights were bold!"

The others were joining in by now. For once the four children were all in complete agreement.

"Put in about tournaments," said Mark.

"And quests," said Jane.

"Put in a good deed, too," said Martha. "Just to be on the safe side."

"Don't forget to say two times everything," said all three. They clustered eagerly around Katharine as she took hold of the charm.

"I wish," said Katharine, "that we may go back twice as far as to the days of King Arthur, and see two tournaments and go on two quests and do two good deeds."

The next thing the four children knew, they were standing in the midst of a crowded highway. Four queens were just passing, riding under a silken canopy. The next moment seven merry milkmaids skipped past, going a-Maying. In the distance a gallant knight was chasing a grimly giant with puissant valor, and in the other direction a grimly giant was chasing a gallant knight for all he was worth. Some pilgrims stopped and asked the four children the way to Canterbury. The four children didn't know.

But by now they were tired of the crowded traffic conditions on the King's Highway, and crossed into a field, where the grass seemed greener and fresher than any they had ever seen in their own time. A tall figure lay on the ground nearby, under an apple tree. It was a knight in full armor, and he was sound asleep.

The four children knew he was asleep, because Martha lifted the visor of his helmet and peeked inside. A gentle snore issued forth.

The knight's sword lay on the ground beside him, and Mark reached to pick it up.

Immediately the sleeping knight awoke, and sat up.

"Who steals my purse steals trash," he said, "but who steals my sword steals honor itself, and him will I harry by wood and by water till I cleave him from his brainpan to his thighbone!"

"I beg your pardon, sir," said Mark.

"We didn't mean anything," said Jane.

"We're sorry," said Katharine.

The knight rubbed his eyes with his mailed fist. Instead of the miscreant thief he had expected to see, he saw Mark and Jane and Katharine and Martha.

"Who be you?" he said. "Hath some grimly foe

murdered me in my sleep? Am I in Heaven? Be ye cherubim or seraphim?"

"We be neither," said Katharine. "And this isn't Heaven. We are four children."

"Pish," said the knight. "Ye be like no children these eyes have ever beheld. Your garb is outlandish."

"People who live in tin armor shouldn't make remarks," said Katharine.

At this moment there was an interruption. A lady came riding up on a milk-white palfrey. She seemed considerably excited.

"Hist, gallant knight!" she cried.

The knight rose to his feet, and bowed politely. The lady began batting her eyes, and looking at him in a way that made the children feel ashamed for her.

"Thank Heaven I found you," she went on. "You alone of all the world can help me, if your name be Sir Launcelot, as I am let to know it is!"

The children stared at the knight, open-mouthed with awe.

"Are you really Sir Launcelot?" Mark asked him.

"That is my name," said the knight.

The four children stared at him harder.

Now that he wasn't looking so sleepy they could see that it was true. No other in all the world could wear so manly a bearing, so noble a face. They were in the presence of Sir Launcelot du Lake, the greatest knight in all the Age of Chivalry!

"How is Elaine?" Katharine wanted to know right away, "and little Galahad?"

"I know not the folk you mention," said Sir Launcelot.

"Oh, yes, you do, sooner or later," said Katharine. "You probably just haven't come to them yet."

"Be ye a prophetess?" cried Sir Launcelot, becoming interested. "Can ye read the future? Tell me more!"

But the lady on the milk-white palfrey was growing impatient.

"Away, poppets!" she said, getting between the four children and Sir Launcelot. "Gallant knight, I crave your assistance. In a dolorous tower nearby a dread ogre is distressing some gentlewomen. I am Preceptress of the Distressed Gentlewoman Society. We need your help."

"Naturally," said Sir Launcelot. He whistled, and his trusty horse appeared from behind the apple tree, where it had been cropping apples. Sir Launcelot started to mount the horse.

The four children looked at each other. They did not like what they had seen of the lady at all, and they liked the way she had spoken to them even less.

Katharine stepped forward.

"I wouldn't go if I were you," she said. "It's probably a trap."

The lady gave her an evil look.

"Even so," said Sir Launcelot, "needs must when duty calls." He adjusted his reins.

Katharine drew herself up to her full four feet four.

"As you noticed before, I be a mighty prophetess!" she cried. "And I say unto you, go not where this lady bids. She will bring you nothing but disaster!"

"I shall go where I please," said Sir Launcelot.

"So there!" said the lady.

"You'll be sorry!" said Katharine.

"Enough of parley," said Sir Launcelot. "Never yet did Launcelot turn from a worthy quest. I know who ye be now. Ye be four false wizards come to me in the guise of children to tempt me from my course. 'Tis vain. Out of the way. Flee, churls. Avaunt and quit my sight, thy bones are marrowless. Giddy-up."

Sir Launcelot chirruped to his horse, and the lady

chirruped to hers, and away they went, galloping down the King's Highway. The four children had to scatter to both sides to avoid the flying hooves.

Of course it was but the work of a moment and a simple problem in fractions for Katharine to wish they all had horses and could follow.

Immediately they had, and they did.

Sir Launcelot turned, and saw the four children close at his heels, mounted now on four dashing chargers.

"Away, fiends!" he said.

"Shan't!" said Katharine.

They went on.

The four children had never ridden horseback before, but they found that it came to them quite easily, though Martha's horse was a bit big for her, and she had trouble posting.

And it was particularly interesting when, every time the lady started casting loving looks at Sir Launcelot, the children would ride up close behind and make jeering noises, and Sir Launcelot would turn in his saddle and shout, "Begone, demons!" at them. This happened every few minutes. Sir Launcelot seemed to get a little bit angrier each time.

When they had ridden a goodly pace they came to

a dark wood, stretching along both sides of the highway. Just at the edge of the wood, the lady cried out that her horse had cast a shoe. Sir Launcelot reined in to go to her aid. The four children stopped at a safe distance.

Then, just as Sir Launcelot was dismounting, three knights rode out of the wood. One was dressed all in red, one in green and one in black. Before the children could cry out, the knights rushed at Sir Launcelot from behind.

It was three against one and most unfair. But even so, Sir Launcelot's strength would have been as the strength of at least nine if he hadn't been taken by surprise. As it was, he had no time even to touch his hand to his sword before the three knights had seized and disarmed him, bound him hand and foot, flung him across the saddle of his own horse, and galloped off into the wood with him, a hapless prisoner.

The lady turned on the four children.

"Ha ha!" she cried. "Now they will take him to my castle, where he will lie in a deep dungeon and be beaten every day with thorns! And so we shall serve all knights of the Round Table who happen this way! Death to King Arthur!"

"Why, you false thing, you!" said Jane.

"I told him so!" said Katharine.

"Let's go home!" said Martha.

"No, we have to rescue him!" said Mark.

"Ho ho!" said the lady. "Just you try it! Your magic is a mere nothing compared with mine, elfspawn! Know that I am the great enchantress, Morgan le Fay!"

"You *would* be!" said Katharine, who didn't like being called "elfspawn," as who would? "I remember you in the books, always making trouble. I wish you'd go jump in the lake!"

Katharine wasn't thinking of the charm when she wished this, or she might have worded it differently. But that didn't stop the charm.

"Good old charm!" said Mark, as he watched what happened.

Morgan le Fay didn't go jump in the lake; she merely fell in a pool. Luckily there was a pool handy. She slid backwards off her horse and landed in it in a sitting position. And luckier still, the pool had a muddy bottom, and Morgan le Fay stuck there long enough for Katharine to make another, calmer wish, which was that she would *stay* stuck, and unable to use any of her magic, for twice as long as would be necessary.

This done, the four children turned their horses into the wood, and set about following the wicked knights. Morgan le Fay hurled a few curses after them from among the water weeds, but these soon died away in the distance.

There was no path to follow through the wood. The branches of trees hung low and thick, and the earth beneath them was damp and dark and dank, and no birds sang.

"This," said Katharine, "is what I would call a tulgey wood."

"Don't!" cried Martha. "Suppose something came whiffling through it!"

The four children pressed on. Suddenly they came to a clearing, and there amidst a tangle of lambkill and henbane and deadly nightshade they saw the witch's castle rising just ahead of them. Poison ivy mantled its walls. There were snakes in the moat and bats in the belfry. The four children did not like the look of it at all.

"What do we do now?" said Jane.

"Wish him free, of course," said Mark.

"Just stand out here and wish? That's too easy!" said Katharine.

"I'm not going inside that castle!" said Martha.

"Nay," said Katharine, who did not seem to be so docile today as she used to be. "Ye forget that I be a mighty prophetess. Trust ye unto my clever strategy!"

"Bushwah," said Mark. "Less talk and more action."

Katharine put her hand on the charm. "I wish that two doors of this castle may stand open for us," she said.

So then the children had to look for the one door that did. They found it at last, a little back door with a small drawbridge of its own, over the moat. The drawbridge was down and the door was ajar. The children went over the drawbridge.

"Beware!" croaked the magic talking frogs in the moat.

They went in through the doorway. A long dark passage lay beyond.

"Beware!" squeaked the magic talking mice in the walls.

The children went along the passage. It wound and twisted a good deal. The magic cobwebs hanging from the ceiling brushed at their faces and caught at their clothing, trying to hold them back, but they broke away and pushed on.

At last the passage ended at a heavy doorway. From beyond it came the sound of loud voices raised in something that was probably intended to be music. The children eased the door open a crack and peeked through, into a large hall.

The red knight and the green knight and the black knight were enjoying a hearty meal, and washing down each mouthful with a draught of nut-brown ale. They were singing at the table, which was rude of them, and the words of their song were ruder still.

> *"Speak roughly to our Launcelot*
> *And beat him with a brier!*
> *And kick him in the pants a lot—*
> *Of this we never tire!*
> *We've put him in a dungeon cell*
> *And there we'll beat him very well!*
> *Clink, canikin, clink!"*

The four children looked at each other indignantly; then they peeked through again.

Some varlets had appeared in the hall. They cleared away the dishes, left the dessert platter on the table, and departed.

The dessert was a number of round plum puddings, all aflame with blazing blue brandy. The black knight stood up to serve them.

At that moment Katharine remembered a story she had once read. She decided to have some fun with the three knights.

"I wish two of those puddings were stuck to the end of your nose!" she cried, putting her hand on the charm and staring straight at the black knight, through the crack of the doorway. And immediately one of them was.

But this pudding, unlike the one in the story, was still burning blue with brandy-fire; so that not only was it humiliating to the black knight, but hurt a good deal as well. And furthermore, his long black whiskers, of which he was inordinately proud, began to singe badly. He gave a wild howl, and his face turned nearly as black as his garments, with rage.

"Ods blood, who hath played this scurvy trick upon me?" he cried, beating at his nose and whiskers with his hands, and then yelling with pain as the flames scorched his fingers.

"Tee hee hee," tittered the green knight. "You look very funny!"

The black knight whirled on him.

"Be it *you,* then, who hath played this scurvy trick?" he cried.

"No, it be not I," said the green knight, "but you look very funny, just the same!"

"Oh, I do, do I?" shouted the black knight, in a passion. And he whipped his sword out of its scabbard, and swapped off the green knight's head.

The red knight jumped to his feet.

"I say, Albemarle, that was going a bit too far!" he cried.

"Oh, I don't know," said the black knight. "He was exceedingly provoking! Come and help me get this great pudding thing off my nose!"

"Well," said the red knight, looking at him rather dubiously, "I don't know if I can, but I'll *try!*"

And he whipped *his* sword out of *its* scabbard, and swapped off the pudding from the black knight's nose. Unfortunately (for him) he swapped off a good bit of the nose, too.

The black knight gave a wild bellow and hurled himself at the red knight, sword in hand. The red knight parried his thrust. A moment later they were joined in deadly combat, leaping about the hall, smashing furniture, and hacking off parts of each other with the greatest abandon.

Behind the door, the four children shut their eyes, held their ears, and cowered trembling in each other's arms.

The combat did not last long. Two sword blades flashed in the air, and a second later two heads fell on the floor, followed, more slowly, by two bodies.

There was a silence. Katharine hadn't meant her wish to end in such a gory and final way. But she reminded herself to be bloody, bold and resolute, and crept through the door into the hall, followed by the three others. All four averted their eyes from what they would have seen if they had looked at the floor.

"I do think you might have managed it neater," said Jane. "How can we get through to the dungeon with all these different pieces of knight lying around underfoot?"

"The point is that I managed it at all," said Katharine, more cheerfully than she felt. "And we don't have to walk; we can wish ourselves there."

She put her hand on the charm and wished that they were twice as far as the dungeon door and that she had two keys to the dungeon in her hand.

After that, of course, it was but a matter of turning the key, and out walked Sir Launcelot, followed by several dozen other knights who had also been prisoners of the enchantress and her friends, and who looked somewhat the worse for their daily beatings.

The other captive knights fell on their knees, kissing the children's hands and hailing them as their deliverers. Sir Launcelot also thanked the children quite politely, but somehow he didn't seem so happy to be free as the children had expected he would.

A moment later, when the other captive knights had left to resume their interrupted quests, the children found out why.

"You saved me by magical means?" Sir Launcelot asked.

"That's right," said Katharine, proudly. "I did it with my little charm."

"That mislikes me much," said Sir Launcelot. "I would it were otherwise."

"Well, really!" said Katharine. "I suppose you'd rather have stayed in there being beaten?"

"Sooner that," said Sir Launcelot, "than bring shame to my honor by taking unfair magical advantage of a foe, however deadly!"

"Well, if you're all that particular," said Katharine, annoyed, "I can easily put them back together again." And she led him into the great hall, and showed him the different pieces of the three knights.

"Please do so," said Sir Launcelot.

"Shall I lock you up in the dungeon again?" asked Katharine, sarcastically. "Doesn't it hurt your conscience that I set you free?"

"That much advantage," said Sir Launcelot, "I think I can take. Some fair jailer's daughter would probably have let me out sooner or later, anyway."

"Oh, is that so?" said Katharine. "I'm sorry I troubled, I'm sure! Is there anything else?"

"Well, yes," said Sir Launcelot. "You might just fetch me my sword and armor, which these cowardly knaves have taken from me."

Thoroughly cross with him by now, Katharine wished the sword and armor back on him; then, working out the fractions carefully, she spoke the wish that was to bring the red knight, the green knight, and the black knight back to life.

It was very interesting watching the different pieces of the different-colored knights reassembling themselves on the hall floor, and the four children were sorry when it was over.

But by then something even more interesting was going on. Because by then Sir Launcelot was fighting the three knights singlehanded, and that was a sight worth coming back many centuries to see.

Sir Launcelot did not seem to appreciate the four children's interest, however.

"Go away. Thank you very much. Good-bye," he called, pinning the green knight against the wall with a table, and holding the red and black ones at bay with his sword.

"Can't we help?" Mark wanted to know.

"No. Go away," said Sir Launcelot, cracking the red knight on the pate, thwacking the black knight in the chest with his backhand swing, and leaping over the table to take a whack at the green one.

"Can't we even *watch?*" Jane wailed.

"No. It makes me nervous. I want to be alone," said Sir Launcelot, ducking under the table to send the red knight sprawling, then turning to face the black and green ones again.

Katharine sighed, and made a wish.

Next moment the four children were on their horses once more, riding along the King's Highway.

"We might at least have waited in the yard," complained Martha. "Now we'll never know how it ended!"

"He'll come out on top; trust *him!*" said Katharine. "I *do* get tired of people who are always right, all the time! Anyway, we'll be seeing him again, I imagine. At the tournament."

"Gee, yes, the tournament. I was forgetting," said Mark. "When do you suppose it'll be?"

"Not for weeks, maybe, by the time here," said Katharine. "But for us, a mere wish on the charm . . ."

And she merely wished.

* * *

"I can't get used to this being rushed around," complained Martha a second later, as she found herself somewhere else for the third time in three minutes. "Where are we now, and when is it?"

"Camelot, I should think," said Katharine, "in tournament time! Look!"

Jane and Mark and Martha looked. Camelot and the field of tournament looked exactly as you all would expect them to look, from the descriptions in *The Boy's King Arthur* and the wonderful books of Mr. T. H. White. Trumpets were blowing clarion calls, and pennons fluttered on the blue air, and armor flashed in the bright light, and gallant knights and trusty squires and faithful pages and ladies fair and lowly varlets were crowding into the stands in hundreds, to watch the chivalrous sport.

The four children had front-row grandstand seats, for Katharine had made that a part of her wish. She had forgotten to say anything in her wish about getting rid of the four horses, and at first these made some trouble by wanting to sit in the grandstand, too, much to the annoyance of the people sitting behind. But Katharine wished them twice as far as away, and they disappeared.

At this, the people behind got up and left in a

hurry, looking back at the four children and muttering about witchcraft and sorcery.

The children paid small heed. They were too busy looking around them and drinking in the sights.

King Arthur sat enthroned on a high platform at one end of the field. The children could see him clearly, with his kind, simple, understanding face, like the warm sun come to shine on merry England. Queen Guinevere was seated at his right, and Merlin, the magician, thin and wise and gray-bearded, at his left.

And now the trumpets blew an extra long fanfare, and the tournament began.

Sir Launcelot was among the first to ride out on the field. The children recognized him by his armor.

"I told you he'd come out all right," said Katharine, a bit bitterly.

But when Sir Launcelot got going in that tournament, even Katharine had to admire him.

He smote down five knights with his first spear, and four knights with his second spear, and unhorsed three more with his sword, until all the people sitting round on the benches began crying out, "Oh, Gramercy, what marvelous deeds that knight doth do in that there field!"

Jane sighed a satisfied sigh. "Kind of glorious, isn't it?" she murmured.

"It's the most wonderful age in human history," said Mark, solemnly. "If only it didn't have to end!"

"Why did it?" asked Martha, who hadn't read *The Boy's King Arthur* yet.

"Partly 'cause some of the other knights got tired of being knocked down all the time and having Launcelot always win," Mark told her.

"Yes," said Katharine, in rather a peculiar voice, "it would really be a good deed, in a way, if somebody knocked *him* down for a change, wouldn't it?"

Mark gave her a sharp look, but just then Sir Launcelot started knocking down more knights, and he had to watch the field. When he looked again, Katharine wasn't there.

Mark nudged Jane hard, as a horrible thought came into his mind.

Jane turned and saw the empty spot where Katharine had been, and Mark could tell that she was having the same thought, too.

Just then there was an interruption in the tournament. A strange knight rode out on the field of combat, and straight up to King Arthur's platform.

"I crave your Majesty's permission to challenge

Sir Launcelot to single combat!" cried the strange knight in a voice loud enough for the children to hear clearly from where they sat.

The hearts of Jane and Mark sank.

Even Martha now guessed the horrid truth. "How dare she?" she whispered.

"I don't know," said Mark. "She's been getting too full of herself ever since we started this wish!"

"Wait till I get her home!" said Jane grimly.

"How call they you, strange sir?" King Arthur was saying, meanwhile, "and whence do you hail?"

"They call me Sir Kath," said the strange knight, "and I hail from Toledo, Ohio."

"I know not this Toledo," said King Arthur, "but fight if you will. Let the combat begin."

The trumpets sounded another clarion call, the strange knight faced Sir Launcelot, and there began the strangest combat, it is safe to say, ever witnessed by the knights of the Round, or any other, Table.

The intrepid Katharine thought herself very clever at this moment. She had wished she were wearing two suits of armor and riding two horses, and she had wished she were two and a half times as tall and strong as Sir Launcelot, and she had wished that she would defeat him twice. And immediately here she was, wearing one suit of armor and riding one horse, and she was one and a quarter times as tall and strong, and she couldn't wait to defeat him once.

But in her cleverness she had forgotten one thing. She had forgotten to wish that she knew the rules of jousting. And here she was, facing the greatest knight in the world, and she didn't know how to start. She knew she'd win in the end, because she'd wished it that way, but what was she to do in the beginning and middle?

Before she could work out another wish to take care of this, Sir Launcelot rode at her, struck her with his lance, and knocked her back onto her horse's tail. Then he rode at her from the opposite direction, and knocked her forward onto her horse's neck.

The crowd roared with laughter.

The feelings of Jane, Mark and Martha may well be imagined.

As for the feelings of Katharine, they knew no bounds. She still held the magic charm clutched in one hot hand, and she wasn't bothering about correct arithmetic now.

"I wish I could fight ten times as well as you, you bully! Yah!" were the words that the valiant Sir Kath spoke, upon the field. It was a cry of pure temper.

And immediately she could fight five times as well as Sir Launcelot, and everyone knows how good *he* was.

What followed would have to be seen to be believed.

Katharine came down like several wolves on the fold. She seemed to spring from all sides at once. Her sword flashed like a living thunderbolt. Her lance whipped about, now here, now there, like a snake gone mad.

"Zounds!" cried the people, and "Lackaday" and "Wurra wurra!"

Jane, Mark and Martha watched with clasped hands.

If Sir Launcelot had not been the greatest knight in the world he would never have lived to tell the tale. Even as it was, the end was swift. In something less than a trice he was unseated from his horse, fell to the ground with a crash, and did riot rise again.

Katharine galloped round and round the field, bowing graciously to the applause of the crowd.

But she soon noticed that the crowd wasn't applauding very loudly. And it was only the traitorous knights like Sir Mordred and Sir Agravaine, the ones who were jealous of Launcelot, who were applauding at all.

The rest of the crowd was strangely silent. For Launcelot, the flower of knighthood, the darling of the people's hearts, the greatest champion of the Round Table, had been defeated!

Queen Guinevere looked furious. King Arthur looked sad. The attendant knights, except for the traitorous ones, looked absolutely wretched. Merlin looked as if he didn't believe it.

Jane and Mark and Martha looked as though they believed it, but didn't want to.

And it was then that the full knowledge of what she had done swept over Katharine.

She had succeeded and she had failed. She, a mere girl, had defeated the greatest knight in history. But she had pretended to herself that she was doing it for a good deed and really it had been just because she was annoyed with Launcelot for not appreciating her help enough, back in Morgan le Fay's castle.

Her cheeks flamed and she felt miserable. It was hot inside her helmet suddenly, and she dragged it off. Then she remembered too late that she'd forgotten something else, when she made her wish. She had wished to be in armor, and to be on horseback, and to be tall and strong, and to win. But she had forgotten to say anything about not being Katharine any longer.

Now, as the helmet came away, her long brown hair streamed down onto her shoulders, and her nine-year-old, little-girl face blinked at the astonished crowd.

Those sitting nearest the ringside saw. Sir Mordred tittered. Sir Agravaine sneered. The mean knights who were jealous of Sir Launcelot began to laugh, and mingled with the laughter were the cruel words, "Beaten by a girl!"

Some horrid little urchins took up the cry, and made a rude song of it:

> *"Launcelot's a chur-ul,"*
> *Beaten by a gir-ul!"*

Sir Launcelot came to, and sat up. He heard the laughter, and he heard the song. He looked at Katharine. Katharine looked away, but not before he had recognized her. He got to his feet. There was silence all round the field; even the mean knights stopped laughing.

Sir Launcelot came over to Katharine. "Why have you done this to me?" he said.

"I didn't mean to," said Katharine. She began to cry.

With flushed cheeks but with head held high, Sir Launcelot strode to King Arthur's platform and knelt in the dust before it. In a low voice he asked leave to go on a far quest, a year's journey away at *least,* that he might hide his shame till by a hundred deeds of valor he would win back his lost honor and expunge the dread words, "Beaten by a girl," forever.

King Arthur did not trust himself to speak. He nodded his consent.

Queen Guinevere did not even look at Sir Launcelot, as he walked away from the field of tournament.

Katharine went on crying.

Merlin spoke a word in King Arthur's ear. King Arthur nodded. He rose, offered an arm to Guinevere, and led her from the stand. Merlin spoke another word, this time to the attendant knights. They began clearing the people from the field.

Most of the people went quietly, but three children in the front row of the grandstand put up quite a fuss, saying that they had to find their sister Katharine, who'd done something terrible, but a sister was a sister and they'd stick up for her, anyway. The knights cleared them away with the rest.

Presently, after what seemed like at least a year, Katharine found herself alone before Merlin. She was still crying.

Merlin looked at her sternly.

"Fie on your weeping," he said. "I wot well that ye be a false enchantress, come here in this guise to defeat our champion and discredit our Table Round!"

"I'm not! I didn't!" said Katharine.

"Ye be, too!" said Merlin, "and you certainly have! After today our name is mud in Camelot!"

"Oh, oh," wept Katharine.

"Silence, sorceress," said Merlin. He waved his wand at her. "I command that you appear before me in your true form!"

Immediately Katharine wasn't tall, or strong, or in armor any more, but just Katharine.

Merlin looked surprised.

"These fiends begin early!" he said. "However, doubtless ye be but the instrument of a greater power." He waved his wand again. "I command that your allies, cohorts, aids, accomplices and companions be brought hither to stand at your side!"

Jane and Mark and Martha appeared beside Katharine, looking nearly as unhappy and uncomfortable as she.

Merlin looked really quite startled. Then he shook his head sadly.

"So young," he said, "and yet so wicked!"

"We're not!" said Martha, making a rude face.

The behavior of the others was more seemly.

"You see, sir," began Mark.

"We didn't mean to," began Jane.

"Let me," said Katharine. "I started it."

And in a rush of words and tears she told Merlin everything, beginning with the charm, and her wish to travel back in time, and going on to what she had hoped to do, and what she'd done and where she'd gone wrong.

"I wanted to do a good deed," she said, "and I *did* one, when I rescued Launcelot from that old dungeon. But then he wasn't properly grateful at all, and made me undo it, so he could rescue himself, all for the sake of his old honor! And that made me cross! And just now I pretended I was defeating him so the other knights wouldn't be so jealous of him, but really I was just trying to get back at him for being so stuck-up! And I always wanted to fight in a real tournament, anyway!"

"Well, now you have," said Merlin, "and what good did you do by it? Just made everybody thoroughly unhappy!"

"I know," said Katharine.

"That's what comes of meddling," said Merlin. "There is a pattern to history, and when you try to change that pattern, no good may follow."

Katharine hung her head.

"However," went on Merlin, and to the surprise of the four children he was smiling now, "all is not lost. I have a few magic tricks of my own, you know. Let me see, how shall I handle this? I *could* turn time back, I suppose, and make it as though this day had never happened, but it would take a lot out of me."

"Really?" said Katharine in surprise. "It would be a mere nothing to *us!*

Merlin looked at her a bit grimly.

"Oh, it would, would it?" he said.

"Oh, yes," went on Katharine happily. "I could wish Launcelot were twice as near as here again, and then I could wish that he'd defeat me twice, and then

I could wish that the people would honor him twice as much as they ever did, and then I could wish . . ."

"Hold!" cried Merlin, in alarm. "A truce to your wishes, before you get us in worse trouble! I think I had best see this wonderful charm of yours." He made a pass at Katharine with his wand. "If there be any magic among you, let it appear now or forever hold its peace."

Katharine's hot hand, which for so long had clutched the charm, opened in spite of itself, and the charm lay in plain sight, on her palm.

Merlin looked at it. His eyes widened. He swept his tall hat from his head, and bowed low before the charm, three times. Then he turned to the children.

"This is a very old and powerful magic," he said. "Older and more powerful than my own. It is, in fact, too powerful and too dangerous for four children, no matter how well they may intend, to have in their keeping. I am afraid I must ask you to surrender it."

He made another pass with his wand. The charm leaped gracefully from Katharine's hand to his own.

Mark spoke.

"But it came to us in our own time," he said, "and that's a part of history, too, just as much as this is.

Maybe we were *meant* to find it. Maybe there's some good thing we're supposed to do with it. There is a pattern to history, and when you try to change that pattern, no good may follow."

Merlin looked at him.

"You are a wise child," he said.

"Just average," said Mark, modestly.

"Dear me," said Merlin. "If that be so, if all children be as sensible as you in this far future time you dwell in . . ." He broke off. "What century did you say you come from?"

"We didn't," said Mark, "but it's the twentieth."

"The twentieth century," mused Merlin. "What a happy age it must be—truly the Golden Age that we are told is to come."

He stood thinking a moment. Then he smiled.

"Very well. Go back to your twentieth century," he said, "and take your magic with you, and do your best with it. But first, I have something to say."

He held the charm at arm's length, rather as though he feared it might bite him, and addressed it with great respect.

"I wish," he said, "that in six minutes it may be as though these children had never appeared here. Except that they—and I—will remember. And I further wish that our tournament may begin all over again and proceed as originally planned by history. Only twice as much so," he added, to be on the safe side.

"Now may I have it back, please?" Katharine asked, when he had done.

"In a minute," said Merlin. "By the way, have you been making a lot of wishes lately? It feels rather worn out to me. It won't last forever, you know."

"Oh dear, we were afraid of that," said Jane. "How many more do we get?"

"That would be telling," said Merlin. "But you'd best not waste too many. It might be later than you think."

"Oh!" cried Martha. "Maybe we'll never get home!"

"Don't worry," said Merlin, smiling at her. "There are still a few wishes left for you. And one more for me." Again he held the charm out before him.

"And I thirdly wish," he said, "for the future protection of the world from the terrible good intentions of these children, and for their protection against their own folly, that this charm may, for twice the length of time that it shall be in their hands, grant no further wishes carrying said children out of their own century and country, but that they may find whatsoever boon the magic may have in store for them in their own time and place." He put the charm into Katharine's hands. "And now you'd best be going. Because in less than a minute by my wish, it will be as though you'd never appeared here. And if you aren't home when that happens, goodness knows where you *will* be!"

"But what about the good deed I wished?" said Katharine. "None of the ones I tried worked out!"

"My child," said Merlin, and his smile was very kind now, "you have done your good deed. You have brought me word that for as far into time as the twentieth century, the memory of Arthur, and of the Round Table, which I helped him to create, will be living yet. And that in that far age people will still care for the ideal I began, enough to come back through time and space to try to be of service to it. You have brought me that word, and now I can finish my work in peace, and know that I have done well. And if that's not a good deed, I should like to know what is. Now good-bye. Wish quickly. You have exactly seventeen seconds."

Katharine wished.

And because their mother and Miss Bick had been

worried yesterday by their being so long away, she put in that when they got home, they should only have been gone two minutes, by real time.

This was really quite thoughtful of Katharine. Perhaps she, too, like Mark the day before, had learned something during her day of adventure.

The next thing the four children knew, they were sitting together in Katharine and Martha's room, and it was still that morning, and they had only been away from home a minute. Yet that minute was packed with memories.

"Did we dream it?" Katharine asked.

"I don't think so, or we wouldn't all remember it," said Mark.

"And we all do, don't we?" said Jane.

And they all did.

"What did that last mean, that Merlin wished on the charm?" Martha wanted to know.

"It means we have to keep our wishes close to home from now on," Mark told her.

"No more travels to foreign climes," said Jane, "and I was all set to take us on a pirate ship next!"

"No more olden times," said Mark, "and I've always wanted to see the Battle of Troy!"

"You might not have liked it, once you got there," said Katharine, from the depths of her experience. "Traveling in olden times is *hard*."

"I don't care," said Martha. "I don't care if I never travel at all. I'm glad to be home. Aren't you?"

And they all were.

5

What Happened to Martha

As a matter of fact, the four children were all so glad to be home that they stayed around the house all the rest of that day.

And that one minute of the morning had been so crowded with adventure that somehow they didn't feel as though they wanted any more excitement for some time.

They put the charm away in its safe place under the flooring, and spent the morning and afternoon playing the most ordinary games they knew, even the tame childish ones that Martha liked and seldom got to play, like Statuary and Old Witch.

At dinner that night, when their mother asked them what they'd been doing all day, they said, "Oh, nothing," and seemed more interested in talking about what *she'd* been doing, at the office.

After dinner there weren't any secret conferences. Instead, the four children prevailed on their mother to join them in a game of Parcheesi.

And when she tired of Parcheesi, as mothers soon will, and offered to read them *A Connecticut Yankee in King Arthur's Court* until bedtime instead, Katharine said quickly that she'd rather hear a good, solid, down-to-normal, everyday book like *Five Little Peppers and How They Grew.*

All this was most unlike the four children.

When they'd finally gone to bed, their mother stole into their various rooms, and felt their foreheads and ears. But none of them had a fever.

The trouble was that the adventure with Sir Launcelot had seemed to point a moral.

And if you have ever had a moral pointed at you, you will know that it is not a completely pleasant feeling. You are grateful for being improved, and you hope you will remember and do better next time, but you do not want to think about it very much just now.

And, as Mark put it next morning, it was a moot question what to do with the charm next. Even wishing to do good deeds with it did not seem to be proof against the occurrence of that hot water in which the four children so often found themselves.

"Of course it has to be just nowadays and in our own country after this," Mark said, "but still! What if we messed up the President and Congress next time, the way we did King Arthur? We could cause a national emergency!"

"I know!" said Jane. "We must proceed with Utter Caution. I've been thinking about it all night, and I'm going to make my next wish really serious. I decided the two things I want most in the world are no more wars and that I knew everything!"

Katharine shook her head doubtfully.

"That's *too* serious," she said. "That's kind of like interfering with God. That might be even worse than trying to change history."

"Is there anything that's serious and fun at the same time?" Martha wondered.

It didn't seem very likely that there was.

And what with this problem, and the horrid

thought that with each wish the charm's power was waning away, and that any day the next wasted wish might be its last, the four children decided to wait until tomorrow before getting on with the serious wishing.

Maybe by tomorrow Jane would have an inspiration. It was her turn next.

Meanwhile today they would have a good old-fashioned day out, the kind of day that had seemed the height of excitement to them, back in the time before the charm had crossed their path. They would put all their allowances together, go downtown on the street car and spend the day, have lunch and see a movie.

To phone their mother and persuade her to tell Miss Bick to let them go was a mere matter of five minutes' wheedling.

Miss Bick made her usual remarks of gloomy foreboding, but the children turned deaf ears, and assembled in Katharine and Martha's room.

"Shall we take it with us or leave it?" Katharine wanted to know.

No one needed to be told what "it" was.

"If we leave it Miss Bick'll be sure to find it," Mark pointed out, "no matter how carefully concealed."

"Think if she made a wish and got half of it!" cried Martha. "What do you suppose it would be?"

"I'd rather not," said Jane. "Some depths are better left unplumbed."

So Jane brought the charm along, wrapped in a special package of old Christmas paper, in her handbag. All the children tied strings around the little finger of each hand, to remind them not to wish for anything, no matter what happened. Then they emerged, and stood waiting at the corner, where they had so often beguiled the summer days by putting pieces of watermelon on the car tracks and waiting for them to squish.

The ride downtown on the street car was uneventful—only the usual trouble between the people who wanted the windows left closed, and the four children, who wanted them open.

Downtown, the children looked in shop windows for a while, then entered that lovely place, the five-and-ten. They bought and ate some saltwater taffy, listened to a young lady play "I Wish I Could Shimmy Like My Sister Kate" on the piano, and bought and ate some parched corn.

It was then time for lunch.

The four children always lunched at the best soda

fountain in town. Today Jane ordered a banana split with chocolate ice cream and raspberry sauce, and Katharine enjoyed a Moonbeam Sundae, thick with pineapple syrup and three kinds of sherbet. Martha always had the same thing, a soda she'd invented, marshmallow with vanilla ice cream, which made the others gag.

There were two things listed on the menu which had intrigued Mark for years. One was called celery soda and the other was called malt marrow, and Mark wondered very much what they could be. Each time he came he promised himself he'd order them next time, but next time his courage always failed. Today he thought of it, thought better of it, and had a double hot fudge dope.

After lunch it was time to choose what movie to see.

The children did this by first making a tour of all the movie theaters in town and looking at the pictures on the outside. A time of argument followed. Mark liked Westerns and thrilling escapes, but Martha wouldn't go inside any theater that had pictures of fighting.

Jane and Katharine liked ladies with long hair and big eyes and tragic stories. They wanted to see a movie called Barbara LaMarr in *Sandra*. Mark finally agreed, because there were a lot of pictures outside of a man who wore a mustache, and that meant he was the villain, and that meant that somebody would hit him sooner or later. Martha agreed because all the other theaters had either pictures with fighting or Charlie Chaplin.

All of the four children hated Charlie Chaplin, because he was the only thing grown-ups would ever take them to.

When they came into the theater Barbara LaMarr in *Sandra* had already reached its middle, and the children couldn't figure out exactly what was happening. But then neither could the rest of the audience.

"But, George, I do not seem to grasp it all!" the woman behind the four children kept saying to her husband.

The four children did not grasp any of it, but Barbara LaMarr had lots of hair and great big eyes, and when strong men wanted to kiss her and she pushed them away and made suffering faces at the audience with her eyebrows, Jane and Katharine thought it was thrilling, and probably quite like the way life was, when you were grown-up.

Mark didn't think much of the love blah, but he watched the villain getting more villainous, and the hero getting more heroic, and patiently waited for them to slug it out.

Martha hated it.

That was always the way with Martha. She wanted to go to the movies like anything until she got there, and then she hated it. Now she kept pestering the others to read her the words and tell her what was happening (for in those days movies did not talk). And when the others wouldn't, she began to whine.

"Be quiet," said Jane.

"I want to go home," said Martha.

"You can't!" said Jane.

"Shush!" said all the other people in the theater.

"I want to, anyway," said Martha.

Jane finally had to put her under the seat. This usually happened in the end.

"Let me out!" said Martha, rising up from below.

But Jane pushed down heavily on the seat, and Martha collapsed under it.

It was dark and gloomy down there, with nothing to look at but dust and old gum other people had got tired of. Martha thought of crying, but she had tried this once in the past, and Jane had kicked her. She decided she might as well go to sleep.

Meanwhile, on the screen above, the hero was finally having his fight with the villain, and Jane and Mark and Katharine forgot all about Martha in their excitement. Jane also forgot to keep hold of her handbag, and it slipped from her lap and fell to the floor.

The wretched Martha, thankful for small favors, took the handbag and put it under her head, though it made rather a lumpy pillow.

I hope it is not necessary to remind you of what was in the handbag.

Jane remembered suddenly, and felt for it, in a panic. It wasn't on her lap. She reached down to feel for it on the floor. At that moment she heard Martha speak.

"Ho hum. I wish I weren't here!" Martha said sleepily.

"Darn!" was the first thought of Jane. "Another wish wasted. Now she'll be only *half* here, I suppose."

Then, as the idea of this sank in, her blood froze. She didn't dare to look. Would just a severed head and shoulders meet her gaze, or would there be only a pair of gruesome legs running around down there?

At last she made herself lean over and see.

The charm hadn't worked it out that way at all. Martha was half there, to be sure, but it was *all* of her that was half there! Her outline was clear, but her features and everything that came between were sort of foggy and transparent. It was as though it were the ghost of Martha that stared up at Jane.

She stared up at Jane and saw her horrified expression; then she stared down at herself. And then Martha—or the half of her that was still there—lost her head completely. Uttering a low wail, she struggled to her feet, scrambled out through the row of seats, and ran up the aisle.

It is not often that one is watching a movie, and suddenly a wailing ghostly figure rises from the floor and scrambles past one.

Most of the ladies Martha scrambled past merely fainted.

The woman who had not grasped it all, before, now gave a shriek, and grasped her husband.

"Oh!" cried Jane, in a rage, catching up her handbag. "I wish I'd never even *heard* of that charm!"

And immediately she had only *half* heard of it. It

was like a story she had read somewhere and half forgotten. And so naturally she didn't think of using the charm to bring Martha back to normal again. Instead, she ran up the aisle after her. Mark and Katharine ran after Jane.

An usher, running down the aisle to see what the coinmotion was, ran into them. He saw the handbag, heard the woman screaming, and decided Jane had stolen the bag. This slowed the children up a little, though no one was seriously hurt. The scratch the usher received was a mere scratch.

Meanwhile the ghostly Martha had run on up the aisle. In the darkness of the theater, not many people noticed her, but in the brightly lit lobby it was another story. The ticket-taker squealed, and threw her tickets in the air. The manager came running out of his office. He saw Martha, and turned pale.

"Oh, what next?" he cried, tearing his hair. "As if business weren't bad enough already, now the theater is *haunted!*" He aimed a blow at her with his cashbox. "Get along with you, you pesky thing!" he cried. "Why don't you go back where you came from?"

The hapless Martha moaned, and flitted on through the lobby, and into the street.

The appearance of her ghostly form upon the

sidewalk caused quite a stir among the city's crowd of shoppers.

"It's an advertising stunt!" said a stout woman. "What they won't think of to sell these here moom pitchers next!"

"It's a sign!" said a thin woman. "It's the end of the world, and me in this old dress!"

"Tell it to go away!" groaned a well-dressed gentleman. "And I'll give back every cent I stole!"

"It's an outrage!" muttered an elderly person. "I shall complain to my Congressman!"

"It's a little girl, only she's only half there," said a child, but of course nobody paid any attention to *her!*

Some people who were afraid of ghosts started running, to get away from the horrible sight.

Martha started running in the opposite direction, to get away from the people.

Other people saw them running, and began to run, too, without knowing why. In no time at all a panic began to spread, as it will when people start behaving in this way, without thinking.

"What's the matter?" said a man to another man who was running by him. "You look as if you'd seen a ghost!"

"I just did!" cried the man. "Look!" And he pointed at the fleeing Martha.

"Don't be silly. There's no such thing," said the first man, who happened to be a learned professor. He glanced at the misty Martha. "Marsh gas," he said. "Very interesting."

"Martians? Did you say Martians?" said a third man, who happened to be passing. "The Martians are invading us!" he cried, without waiting for an answer. He began to run and everyone who heard him began running, too.

By the time Jane and Mark and Katharine had dealt with the usher and emerged from the movie theater, pandemonium reigned in the street. Someone had called the fire department and turned in a general alarm. Someone else had telephoned the police and asked them to send the riot squad. The wails of approaching fire sirens and the screeches of police whistles added confusion to the scene.

A crowd of people rushed past the theater.

"The Martians have landed!" they cried, pointing back in the opposite direction. "We saw one of them, all transparent and horrible!"

Jane and Mark and Katharine looked up the street

in the direction the people were pointing in. Far in the distance they could just make out the dim figure of Martha, running along all by herself. They ran after her.

By this time no one was paying any attention to Martha at all. Everyone was too busy worrying about imaginary men from Mars.

But somehow, once she had started running, Martha found that she couldn't stop. And the more she ran, the more frightened she felt. This often happens.

She came to a corner, and turned it. The noise of the shouting and the sirens died away behind her. She was in a quiet street she had never seen before, a street of little shops. The street was deserted. Martha chose the middle shop and went in.

A few seconds later Jane and Mark and Katharine came round the corner and stood looking at the little shops. There was no sign of any part of Martha.

"Use the charm!" Mark cried. "Wish!"

"Oh, that old story!" said Jane. "Who ever believed that?"

Mark and Katharine stared at her with open mouths.

"What did you say?" said Mark.

Jane didn't answer. Quickly making up her mind, she chose a shop at one end of the row, and started in. Mark and Katharine, wondering what in the world had happened to Jane, followed. Then the three children stopped in the doorway, horrified.

The shop was a jeweler's, and costly diamonds and rich rings glittered on its counters. In the shop were a man and a woman. The man had a cap pulled low over his eyes. The woman wore a black-and-white skirt and a red blouse.

"Come on," the man was saying. "Now's de chance to loot de joint while everybody's away watchin' de riot!"

The man and woman started loading their pockets with pieces of jewelry from the counter. Katharine chose this moment to sneeze. The man and woman turned, and saw the three children standing in the doorway.

The man with the cap advanced toward Jane in a menacing fashion.

"O.K.," he said. "Hand over de bag."

Jane clutched her handbag to her. She seemed to half remember that there was a particular reason why she shouldn't lose it, but she couldn't think what the reason was. She didn't know what to do.

But Mark knew. He put his hand on the bag Jane was holding, and wished he and Jane and Katharine were where Martha was, only twice as far.

The next moment the man in the cap and the woman in the red blouse were alone, looking at the spot where the three children had been.

"Jeepers creepers!" said the man in the cap. "Dey've flew de coop!"

When Martha ran into the middle shop, at first she didn't see anybody, only books.

There were books in shelves on all the walls, and books on tables in all the corners. There was a large desk in the middle of the shop, piled high with books, and at first that seemed to be all. Then a face peered at Martha from over the pile of books on the desk, and a second later a rather small gentleman emerged from behind it. The gentleman wore a small pointed beard, and he held an open book in one hand.

He looked at Martha.

Martha looked back at him, waiting for him to scream, or faint, or run away, the way everyone else had.

But the rather small gentleman did none of these things. He smiled, and bowed politely.

"Good afternoon," he said. "I presume this is a ghostly visitation? I am honored. Did you come out of one of the books? You might be Little Nell, I suppose, or Amy March, though the clothes don't look right."

"No, I'm Martha," said Martha. "And I didn't come out of a book; I came by magic charm."

And although she was old enough by now to know that no grown-up ever will credit any story that has magic in it, she proceeded to tell the small gentleman all about the charm, starting from the beginning. The small gentleman seemed particularly interested in the part about the children's mother.

"This didn't happen out on West Bancroft Street, by any chance, did it?" he interrupted her to ask. "About three nights ago?"

"Why, yes! How did you know?" said Martha, amazed.

"Never mind," said the small gentleman. "Do go on. Tell me more."

So Martha told him all about the movies, and Jane's putting her under the seat, and the wish she had made, and all that had happened afterwards.

"And so here I am," she ended, "only I'm only half here."

"So I see," said the small gentleman.

"It's kind of an interesting feeling, now I'm not scared anymore," said Martha. "Only I'm about ready for it to stop now. Mother'll be expecting us by dinnertime, and I'm afraid she might not like it if I came home like this. She isn't good with magic, the way you are. It upsets her."

"Yes, I know it does," said the small gentleman, absently.

"Oh, do you know Mother?" said Martha.

"Well, not exactly," said the small gentleman.

"Then how do you know about her? Are you magic, too? Are you a wizard or something? I thought you might be, when I saw that beard. Do you know any tricks to put me back together again?"

"I'm afraid not," said the small gentleman.

"Of course if Mark and Jane and Katharine were here," Martha went on, "they've got the charm, and they could wish me back. Don't you have any spells to sort of summon people?"

The small gentleman shook his head. "No spells. And I'm not a wizard, I'm sorry to say. This is the first magic thing that ever happened to me, though I always hoped something would. But maybe we can find them by regular means. What did they do when you ran out of the theater? Did they run after you?"

Martha looked startled. "Why!" she said. "I never even thought to look back!"

"They probably did," said the small gentleman. "They've probably been following you all the time. They're probably outside the shop right now, looking for you!"

"I'll go see," said Martha, starting for the door.

And it was at that exact moment that Mark, in the jewelry store down the street, made the wish that was to take him and Jane and Katharine to Martha's side. Immediately they were there.

"I did it!" said Martha. "I found them!"

"No, you didn't. Mark wished on the charm," said Katharine.

"I don't see why you all keep talking like that," said Jane. "There's no such thing as charms."

"Oh?" said the small gentleman. "That's not what your sister's been telling me."

"Who are you?" said Jane, rudely.

"Quiet," said Mark. "This is no time for mere bickering. We've got to fix up what we did. We've got to stop that awful panic. It's terrible—we were going to be so careful, and look what happened! You'd think that charm would have better sense!"

"There is no charm," said Jane.

"Stop saying that," said Mark. "Listen!"

The distant sound of fire sirens and police whistles and a cry of people could be heard.

"Now that you mention it," said the small gentleman, "I *did* think I noticed some slight disturbance, earlier."

"Slight," said Mark, "is not the word. Compared with the events of today, the Johnstown Flood will go down in history as a mere trifle!"

"I know it's my fault for wishing that wish," said Martha, "but I think it's everybody else's fault, too. Why did they all have to get so excited and start running?"

"One of the least admirable things about people," said the small gentleman, "is the way they are afraid of whatever they don't understand."

"And by now thousands are probably killed or homeless," went on Mark, drearily, "and burglars on every hand looting the deserted city! And Mother knows we're downtown!" he added, as a new thought struck him. "She'll be worried, and out looking for us!"

"If I may make a suggestion," said the small gentleman, "now if ever is a time for a really good wish."

"I'd be ashamed," said Jane. "Misleading these innocent children, pretending you believe in it!"

"Oh, what's the matter with her? Stop her, somebody!" said Katharine.

"Let me," said Martha. "I got us into this. I ought to get us out."

She tried to take the handbag from Mark. But of course the handbag just fell through her misty hand onto the floor. So then Mark held the bag, and Martha draped herself against it, in a clinging, clammy sort of way, like fog against a windowpane, as Katharine afterwards put it, and wished that Jane might be twice cured of whatever it was that ailed her. And right away Jane remembered about the charm.

The next wish was that their mother might find them safe and sound in four minutes' time.

"That gives me two minutes," said Martha, "to put myself back together in." For the third time she draped herself against the bag. "I wish," she began.

But there was an interruption.

Some people had appeared in the doorway of the shop. It was the man in the cap and the woman in the red blouse. Their pockets were bulging, probably with ill-gotten loot. The man looked round at the walls of bookshelves.

"Dis joint ain't no good, Mae," he said. "Dey ain't got nothin' but books."

"May I help you?" asked the small gentleman, stepping forward.

"How could you help me, if you ain't got nothin' but books?" said the man. Then he broke off, as he saw the four children. "Well, if it ain't de vanishin' marvels!" he said. "Kids, you got some disappearin' act! You carry it in dat bag?"

"What bag?" said Mark, putting the handbag behind him.

The man had seen Martha now.

"What's de matter wid *her*?" he said. "She get stuck half disappeared?" Then he smiled grimly. "O.K.," he said. "Tricks like dem I can use. Hand over de bag."

"I won't," Mark started to say, bravely. But before he could say it, the man snatched the bag from his hands and turned to run.

For the second time that afternoon Mark made

a wish in the very nick, in the words of Katharine. He dove at the man in a flying tackle, and as the two of them went down together, he touched the bag and wished that he might capture the thieves singlehanded.

Of course one-half as good as singlehanded is double-handed; so it took him both hands to do it.

But thirty seconds later, when the two minutes were up and the children's mother walked into the bookshop, a startling scene met her gaze.

A male and a female thief lay bound and gagged on the floor, while Mark stood over them victoriously, his hands dripping diamonds and rubies.

Watching him in admiration were Jane and Katharine and Martha, only Martha seemed to be completely transparent.

And perhaps oddest of all, there stood the rather small gentleman with the beard who had given her a lift on the night she visited Uncle Edwin and Aunt Grace and had the strange adventure.

The combination of all these surprises, after the worry she had had during the panic in the streets, proved too much for her. She stood swaying in the doorway for a moment, a prey to conflicting emotions. Then she tottered to a chair and collapsed.

Like many another in that unfortunate city, during the half hour since Martha made her first wish, she had fainted.

The small gentleman bent over her and chafed her wrists.

"She'll be all right, won't she?" Martha asked, anxiously.

"I think so. I'm sure so," said the small gentleman.

"Good. To work, then," said Martha. And she draped herself against the handbag and wished that she might be twice as much there as she ever was.

"That's better," she said, a moment later, looking down at her old, solid self with satisfaction. Then she took the handbag firmly in her own substantial hand, and wished that the man in the cap and the woman in the red blouse might become twice as reformed in their characters as any two thieves had ever yet become.

Mark and Katharine unbound and ungagged the two thieves.

"Oh, what a wicked one I went and been," said the man in the cap. "Now I'm sorry."

"I been twice as wicked as you was," said the woman in the red blouse. "I'm twice as sorry, too!"

"You ain't," said the man in the cap. "You ain't capable."

Tiring of this, Martha wished them twice as far as where they belonged, and they went away, probably to join the Salvation Army.

The next thing was to wish the stolen jewelry all back where it belonged, too, and this was a simple problem. Then came a harder one.

"I wish," said Martha, "that anybody who's been hurt or upset, or anything that's been broken, or gone wrong because I wished that wish, may be twice as good as it was before. And I wish that everything that has happened because I made that wish should go right out of everybody's mind, and be as though it were a dream. Only twice as much so."

"Except me, please," said the small gentleman. He was standing looking down at their mother in rather an odd way. "I should hate not to remember every bit of this afternoon."

"Except," Martha began. Then she broke off. "What's your name?"

"Smith," said the small gentleman.

"Except Mr. Smith," said Martha. "And us, too, of course," she added.

They stood listening.

In the distance the sound of the fire sirens and the police whistles and the crowd broke off suddenly. There was a silence. Then faintly, the normal roar of city traffic, usually so ugly, but for this one time so beautiful to hear, fell on their charmed ears.

Martha relaxed with a sigh.

"I was afraid it might wear out before it got through that one," she said.

"It was a pretty big wish," Mark agreed. "It must have been quite a strain on it. Maybe that'll be the last wish we get."

"Let's wait a while before we find out," said Katharine.

Their mother stirred, and opened her eyes. She looked around her.

"Where am I?" she said, just like fainted people in books. Then she saw the four children, and held out her arms.

The three girls ran to her. So, even though he was a boy, did Mark.

"I had such a terrible dream," their mother said. "I dreamed there was an awful panic in the city, and I was out in it, looking for you, and then—"

"And then you came into my shop and found them," said Mr. Smith.

127

Their mother looked at him.

"It really is you," she said.

"Yes," he said.

"But I thought—" their mother began.

"I could have sworn—" she began again.

She passed her hand over her forehead, and smiled rather palely at Mr. Smith. "Every time we meet I seem to think something strange has just happened!"

She got to her feet and looked round the room again.

"There really weren't any thieves or diamond necklaces, were there?" she said.

"What?" said Mark.

"You must have dreamed it," said Martha.

"I think I'd better go home and lie down," said their mother. "I feel very peculiar."

"Ahem," said Mr. Smith, clearing his throat nervously. "I have a better idea. Couldn't you all come out to dinner with me? We could go to a movie or something afterwards."

"We really couldn't," said their mother. "And yet I think I'd like to," she added suddenly, in rather a surprised voice.

"Only no movies, please," said Martha.

"Well, then," said their mother, rather shyly, "per-

haps we could all go out to our house after dinner."
She looked at Mr. Smith, and laughed. "We seem to
be fated to know each other better!" she said.

And perhaps they were.

Because that's what they did.

6

What Happened to Jane

The dinner with Mr. Smith and the evening that followed were an almost complete success. And the biggest success of the evening, for Mark and Katharine and Martha, was Mr. Smith himself.

The four children generally divided all grown-ups into four classes. There were the ones like Miss Bick and Uncle Edwin and Aunt Grace and Mrs. Hudson who—frankly, and cruel as it might be to say it—just weren't good with children at all. There was nothing to do about these, the four children felt, except be as polite as possible and hope they would go away soon.

Then there were the ones like Miss Mamie King, who—when they were with children—always seemed to want to pretend *they* were children, too. This was no doubt kindly meant, but often ended with the four children's feeling embarrassed for them.

Somewhat better were the opposite ones who went around treating children as though the children were as grown-up as they were, themselves. This was flattering, but sometimes a strain to live up to. Many of the four children's school teachers fell into this class.

Last and best and rarest of all were the ones who seemed to feel that children were children and grown-ups were grown-ups and that was that, and yet at the same time there wasn't any reason why they couldn't get along perfectly well and naturally together, and even occasionally communicate, without changing that fact.

Mr. Smith turned out to be one of these.

He allowed, and even urged, the four children to choose anything they wanted from the menu at dinner, at the same time frankly advising Mark that he thought he would enjoy rare steak and fried onions more than he would codfish tongues.

Jane said she wasn't very hungry, and would her mother order something for her, please? And no, she didn't think she cared for any dessert, thank you. The other three stared at her in disbelief.

After dinner came the ride home, and that was exciting, for everyone did not own a motor car in those days, and the four children were among the ones who didn't. Mr. Smith showed them the way to shift from high into second without stopping, and Mark thought this almost as magical as anything the charm had done for them so far.

Jane said she had seen it before. The other three thought this rude of her.

When they arrived at home Mr. Smith proved an adept player of Fan Tan and I Doubt It, and when card-playing palled was enthralling in his description of his travels in Darkest Australia.

Jane said she was tired and didn't feel like playing games or talking, and she guessed she'd go to bed and finish *Hildegarde's Harvest* instead. The other three looked at each other, and decided they had better have a word with Jane later on.

But when at last, very late, they were sent to bed, and stopped to peek into her room, she was asleep, or pretending to be.

And the next morning they didn't get a chance to ask her what had been the matter, because the next morning was Saturday and Saturday mornings in that house were always a thing of frenzy.

On Saturdays the children's mother came home from work early, and Miss Bick stayed only a half day, and those were two good things about Saturday.

But on Saturdays Miss Bick always seemed bent on cramming a whole day's fussing and nagging into one morning, and today the four children were kept so busy polishing silver and cleaning out bureau drawers and dusting and doing errands that they scarcely had time to exchange a word if two of them met by chance in the hall.

So it wasn't until along toward lunchtime that one or two, and finally three and four were able to gather together in Katharine and Martha's room and examine the outlook of the day.

The outlook of the day naturally hinged on the charm, and what they were going to do with it next.

"There's one thing bothers me," Martha was saying to Katharine, as Mark and then Jane joined them. "When I was only half there, where did the other half of me go?"

"Don't," said Katharine. "That's one of those questions that give you a headache just to think about. Like which came first, the chicken or the egg."

"All the same," said Mark, sitting down next to them, "it might be fun to find out."

"You mean wish ourselves there?" Katharine's eyes were round. "Wherever it is?"

"I don't want to!" said Martha. "It might be just nowhere at all! We might be just nothingness!"

"If we were, we wouldn't know it," Mark pointed out.

"But that's *worse!* Then we'd never get back at all!" Martha cried, getting excited. "I don't *want* to not know it! I don't want to be just nothingness! If we wish that, I won't come!"

"Well, you won't have to because we aren't going to!" said Jane, speaking for the first time. She walked over to the secret place and took out the charm. "It's my turn next and I don't feel like wishing. I may not make a wish for years and years. If ever." And putting the charm in her pocket, she started for the door.

"What's the matter with you?" said Mark, getting up to follow.

"Oh, nothing at all!" said Jane, turning on him. "Not a thing! Everything's just wonderful! Everything's just fine and dandy! Everything's just hunky-dory!"

"Well, isn't it?" asked Katharine.

"Everything's just spoiled, that's all!" Jane cried. "Everything's just utterly and completely ruined! All because some people have to tell everything they know!" And she glared at Martha.

"What did I do?" said Martha.

"As if you didn't know!" said Jane. "Here I thought we were going to have a wonderful, exciting, secret summer full of thrilling adventures, and you had to go and tell the whole thing to the first old stranger that came along!"

"You mean Mr. Smith?" said Martha, surprised. "He's not a stranger anymore. He's a friend."

"Oh, he is, is he?" said Jane. "That makes it all just lovely, doesn't it? And now I suppose we'll have grown-ups butting in and telling us what to wish all the time, and like as not wanting to borrow the charm and wasting its substance on their own devices

and desires, and it's just all utterly and completely ruined!" And she went down the hall and into her own
room and shut the door.

The others stared after her, amazed.

"Doesn't she like Mr. Smith?" said Martha.

"No," said Mark. "I don't think she does."

In her room Jane sat on the bed and gave way to
gloom. She felt awful inside, the way you always do
when you've been perfectly hateful to those you love
best, and she didn't even know why she had done
it. She didn't know why the mere thought of Mr.
Smith upset her so — or if she did know the reason
she didn't want to admit it, even to herself.

But the thing was that Jane was the only one of
the four children who really remembered their father.

Martha was only a baby when their father died,
and Katharine and even Mark were still very young,
too young for them to recall very much about him
now. But Jane remembered him clearly and with a
great deal of love, and for that reason she couldn't
bear the thought of Mr. Smith's coming into their
lives and getting to know them better and better,

and finally growing to be just like one of the family, and even trying to take the place of a father to them, which was what she was perfectly sure Mr. Smith hoped to do.

So now she sat in her room and thought and thought, and felt thoroughly miserable. Even the presence of the charm in her pocket was no comfort, because while it would serve the others right if she made a wish all by herself, the only wishes she could think of to make were horrible murderous ones, and she was old enough and nice enough to know that wishing herself invisible and going and pulling Mr. Smith's beard, or writing him a threatening letter with a pen dipped in blood wouldn't really be a bit of help or make her feel a bit better.

After a few minutes there was a knock at the door, and Mark and Katharine and Martha trooped in, looking solemn.

"We've been thinking," Mark said, "and we thought we ought to hold a Council."

"About Mr. Smith," said Martha.

"Go away," said Jane.

"You'd like him if you really got to know him," said Mark. "He was lots of fun last night."

"Humph!" said Jane.

"He was a big help when I wasn't all there," said Martha. "He's sensible about magic, not like most grown-ups at all."

"Ha!" said Jane.

"So we were thinking," said Katharine, and then trailed off, looking at Mark.

"Well?" said Jane.

"You tell her," said Katharine to Mark.

"We were thinking," said Mark, "that maybe before we make another wish we ought to go see Mr. Smith and sort of ask his advice. Just in a general way."

"*What?*" said Jane.

"I think we ought to take him along in the wish *with* us," said Martha. "Then he could help us out again if we get in more trouble!"

"The way we always seem to," said Katharine.

"Then you could really get to know him," said Mark.

"And everything would be all right again," said Martha.

Jane was looking at them as if she couldn't believe her ears. "Has everyone in this family gone utterly and completely *insane?*" she cried. "Don't you know why he's so interested in us and nice about things?

Haven't you seen the way he and Mother keep looking at each other? Do you want some old *stepfather*
moving in here and changing everything?"

The others looked surprised at this, but not really
terribly shocked.

"I should think he might make kind of an ideal
one," said Katharine.

"It's good for a growing boy, having a man around
the house," said Mark.

"I've always wished I had a father," said Martha.

Jane began to storm. "Do you really think he could
ever take Father's place? Him and his old beard! Don't
you know what stepfathers always turn out to be like,
once the fatal deed is done? Don't you remember Mr.
Murdstone? Oh!" she cried, glaring round at them
all. "It's no use! You don't understand! I wish . . ."

She broke off in alarm, remembering the charm.
Then, a prey to utter recklessness, she plunged her
hand into her pocket, grasped the charm firmly, and
went on. "Yes, I do! I wish I belonged to some other
family! I wish it twice!"

Mark and Katharine and Martha gasped. This was
the worst thing that had happened yet. They hardly
dared look at Jane, for fear she might start turning
into someone else before their eyes.

But when they did look, there stood the same brown-haired, blue-eyed, snub-nosed Jane they had grown to know and love through the years. Nothing seemed to have happened. Maybe nothing had. Mark decided to find out.

"Look here, old Jane-ice," he said, putting his hand on her arm and using a pet name that was reserved for unusual serious moments. "You didn't mean it, did you?"

"You let me go, you bully!" remarked a prim, lady-like voice none of the children had ever heard before in their lives. "You horrid big boy! I don't like boys! And I don't like *you!*"

"Oh!" cried Martha, turning pale. "She doesn't know us!"

"Of course she does," said Katharine. "You know *me,* don't you, dear? Kathie, that you've been through thick and thin with?"

"No. I don't know you and I don't wish to. Your frock is soiled," said the voice that, to their horror, seemed to be coming out of Jane. "My mama told me never to play with strange children."

Martha began to sniff.

"What an insanitary little girl," said the voice. "Tell her to use a handkerchief. She'll give me a germ."

"Oh, what's the matter with her?" Martha's voice rose to a wail.

"It's not her fault," Katharine said, trying to be reassuring for Martha's sake. "It's the way she's been brought up, I suppose. By that other family she belongs to, now. It *does* show what a good influence we've been, doesn't it? She was lots nicer under our tender care."

"I don't believe it," said Mark. "She's just trying to fool us, aren't you, Jane-ice?"

"Don't call me that," said the voice. "That's not my name."

"All right, then," said Mark, turning on her suddenly. "If that isn't your name, what is?"

The strange girl who looked like Jane, yet was Jane no longer, seemed startled for a moment, as if she weren't quite sure of the answer. Then her face cleared.

"My mother calls me her Little Comfort," she said.

Mark made a gagging noise.

Katharine looked disgusted. "To think one of us should have come to this!" she mourned.

"It would be an errand of mercy to put the poor thing out of her misery," Mark agreed.

141

She-who-was-no-longer-Jane was staring around the room.

"I don't like this house," she said. "The furnishings are in poor taste. It is gaudy." Her lower lip began to tremble. "I want to go home."

"Oh, you do, do you?" said Mark. "Well, I can fix that. No sooner said than done." And he made a dive for the pocket where he knew the charm lay concealed.

But She (who was no longer Jane) pulled away, and gave him a surprisingly hard slap for such a miminy-piminy, ladylike type.

"Take that!" she cried. "You are a thief, as well as a bully!" She glared round at them all. "You are a lot of badly-brought-up children. You kidnapped me, and then tried to rob me. I'm going to tell my mother!"

And with these words, she flounced out into the hall and started down the stairs. By the time the others had recovered from their shock and dashed after her, she was in the act of mincing out the front door.

Mark and Katharine took the stairs three at a time. Martha used the banister. But in the lower hall Miss Bick leaped forth and barred the way.

"No, you don't!" she said. "Not a soul leaves this house until the table's set for lunch!"

There was nothing the children could do about this, and nothing that they felt prepared to say. They didn't even point out that Jane had already left. As Katharine said afterwards, the way Jane was acting, right then she probably didn't *have* a soul!

But never was table set with such wild abandon, never did silver fly through the air with such great ease as it then flew. Hardly more than one precious minute had been wasted in idle drudgery before Mark and Katharine and Martha rushed out the front door and down the steps onto the sidewalk, and stood scanning the offing in all directions.

Far down Maplewood Avenue they could just make out a genteel figure in Jane's dress, picking its way along and toeing out in a way that the real Jane would have scorned to be seen doing in public. As they watched, the figure turned to the right, into Virginia Street.

And as they started to dash after it, a car drove up before the house, and Mr. Smith got out and held the door open for their mother.

"Company for lunch!" their mother called,

blushing pink and looking embarrassed and pretty. "Where's Jane?"

The three children looked at each other and then quickly looked away again.

"We don't know, *exactly*," said Katharine.

"We think she's visiting somebody over on Virginia Street," said Mark, hoping that he spoke the truth, and that She (who was all that was left of Jane) had not strayed farther.

"Well, go and get her," said their mother, taking some interesting-looking packages from the car. "This is a party."

The three children looked at the ground, hopelessly.

"Or wait," their mother went on, not noticing. "You all go in the car and pick her up; that'll be quicker. I'll be breaking the news to Miss Bick about the party." And she started toward the house, her arms loaded with packages.

Mark and Katharine and Martha waited till she was safely inside. Then they turned to Mr. Smith and all started to speak at once. Then they stopped and looked at each other again.

"Shall we tell him?" Katharine asked.

"Yes." Mark nodded decisively. "There comes a time in the affairs of men, and this is it."

"I *said* we ought to, all along," said Martha. "I said he'd know what to do. This'll prove it."

And she and Mark and Katharine all piled into the front seat of the car and began telling Mr. Smith about the dread events of the morning. They didn't go into the reason for Jane's upset, though, or the way she felt about stepfathers, out of consideration for his feelings.

And Mr. Smith didn't waste time in unnecessary questions. ("Which proves," said Mark to Katharine, afterward, "that he would make an ideal step, and not Murdstone at all!") He started the motor, and the car shot down Maplewood and turned into Virginia Street.

She-who-was-no-longer-Jane was no longer to be seen.

"She must be in this block somewhere," said Katharine. "She hasn't had time to walk any farther."

"What do we do now?" said Martha.

"The question is moot," said Mark. "She could be in any one of these houses."

"We could holler 'Fire!' and everyone would come running out," suggested Katharine.

"Let's not have any more fires or running." Martha shuddered, remembering certain past experiences. "Let's knock at all the doors and ask them if they want to subscribe to the *Literary Digest*."

"That's no good," said Mark, who had done this one summer to try to earn spending money. "All they ever say is 'No,' and shut the door."

Martha turned to Mr. Smith. "It's up to you," she said trustingly.

Mr. Smith looked pleased and touched. He also looked a little nervous, as though he were hoping he might live up to their trust. He cleared his throat.

"Well," he said, "first of all, does any of these houses look like the kind of house the family of that kind of girl would live in?"

Mark and Katharine and Martha stared up and down the block. Luckily it was a short one, with only eight houses in it, four on each side of the street. Almost all the houses looked very much like their own—comfortable, slightly shabby, family sort of houses, with an easy-to-get-along-with, lived-in look.

All but one.

The eighth house was made of cold-looking gray stone, and sat primly on an impossibly neat emerald lawn that was shut off from the street by a forbidding hedge of evergreens. A small sign on the lawn said "Please." The walk to the front door was of bright blue gravel, edged with some boring plants that looked as though they had never blossomed and didn't intend to. There were no croquet wickets on the lawn and no bicycles or kiddy-cars sitting around, the way there were in front of most of the other houses.

"That's the one." Mark was positive. "It has to be. It looks just like her."

He and Katharine and Martha and Mr. Smith got out of the car and advanced stealthily up the street till they stood confronting the gray stone house. No one was in sight. From within came the sound of someone practicing a difficult piece upon the piano.

"That couldn't be Jane," said Martha. "She hates practice."

"I bet she doesn't now," said Mark.

"We'd better not let her see *us*," said Katharine. " She doesn't seem to like us very well any more."

"If her new family's anything like her, I don't think *they'll* like us either," said Mark. He turned to Mr. Smith. "I guess it's still up to you, sir."

Mr. Smith cleared his throat nervously again. "All right," he said. "I'll try."

So Mark and Katharine and Martha hid behind the evergreen hedge, and Mr. Smith, after checking to make sure that no telltale parts of them were exposed to the public gaze, squared his shoulders and marched bravely up the blue gravel walk and knocked on the front door with the imitation antique brass knocker.

When She-who-was-no-longer-Jane turned out of Maplewood into Virginia Street, she went straight to the gray stone house and up the blue gravel walk, and in at the front door. After all, this was her house and she belonged to this family now.

She went in at the front door and up the front stairs to what was now her room. There were handwoven curtains of a cold gray at the windows, and the walls were painted in the same colorless tint. There were no colored pictures on the walls, only sepia prints of Sir Galahad and a lady called Hope. The bookshelves were full of heavy, instructive-looking books, and no toys or games, only a few sets of the helpful kind that show you how to weave linen and tool leather in six easy lessons.

She-who-was-no-longer-Jane sat down on an uncomfortable imitation antique chair and began looking at one of the instructive books. She did this as though it were perfectly natural and as though she'd been doing nothing else for years, but all the same, deep down inside her, she felt strangely empty and uncomfortable, as though she didn't belong in this prim gray room at all.

After a bit, deciding she didn't feel like being instructed just now, she put down the book and took a round, shining object from her pocket. She sat staring at it for a long while. In a dim way her mind connected it with the empty, uncomfortable feeling that seemed to hang over her, but she couldn't remember why the shiny thing made her feel lonely and unhappy.

Of course the trouble was that when she wished to belong to another family, she hadn't said a thing about not being Jane any longer. And so she had become the girl Jane would have been if she had been brought up in this cold, gray house. But down inside her somewhere, the real Jane was still struggling to exist. This is called heredity versus environment, and it is quite a struggle.

After she had been sitting by herself (or by her

two selves) for a few minutes, a lady appeared in the door. She was dressed in a gown of sober gray wool.

"Why, here you are!" she cried. "Mother has been worried. She couldn't find her Little Comfort anywhere!"

"I was playing," said She-who-was-now-part-Jane and-part-Mother's-Little-Comfort (only from now on I think it will save time if we just think of her as She).

"Where were you playing?" said the gray lady. "You weren't in the solarium and you weren't in the patio!"

"I was around the corner. I was playing with some children."

"But we don't know anyone around the corner," said the gray lady in alarm. "Mother wants you to have fresh air and exercise, of course, but one can't be too careful about speaking to strangers! Were they nice children?"

She hesitated. "*You* wouldn't like them," She said, finally, hanging her head and looking closer at the round shining thing in her hand.

"Really, Comfort, you are not behaving like yourself today!" said the lady, reproachfully.

"I know it," said She, unhappily.

"Haven't I told you always to look at me when I am speaking to you?" the lady went on. "What is that you have in your hand?"

"I don't know. I found it."

"Let me see," said the lady. She took the shining thing in her own hand. "But this is very interesting! It seems to be some kind of ancient talisman. See, there is writing on it, but I don't recognize the language. It is not Greek or Latin. Probably it is Sanskrit. Father will translate it for us when he comes home. And now how would you like to take a nice nap until dinnertime?"

Jane and Mark and Katharine and Martha had all scorned naps for years, and the small remnant of Jane that was still there somewhere, buried under layers, of Little Comfort, rose to the surface. "I wouldn't like it at all," She said.

"But you always have a nap at this hour!" cried the lady.

"Do I?" said She, her heart sinking. "Couldn't I dig some worms and go fishing instead?"

The lady looked shocked. "Why, Comfort! You know fishing is cruel, except when necessary to provide food, and we are all vegetarians here!"

"Build a block fort and have a war with toy soldiers?" suggested She, faintly.

"Why, Comfort!" cried the lady again. "There are no toy soldiers in this house! They are symbols of world militarism, and not suitable playthings! I can't think what has come over you today! It must be the influence of those bad children! No, let us go down to the drawing room and put this ancient talisman in the curio cabinet, and then you can practice your new piece till Father comes."

The remnant of Jane that still existed didn't like seeing the round shining thing go out of her possession at all, and she didn't much want to practice a new piece either. And she had her doubts about a house in which naps were taken and bright colors were shunned, and things that were ordinary and fun were made to seem ugly and wicked. But She dejectedly followed the gray lady out of the room and down the stairway into the drawing room, which was large and cold and grey, and took her seat on the piano stool.

And it turned out that practicing on the piano, which was always sheer torment to Jane in the past, was a mere cinch now. She played away primly and perfectly, while the gray lady sat in a stiff chair of carved oak, and looked at a magazine called *The Outlook*.

This went on for what seemed like years, and the last trace of Jane was just beginning to think it might as well die away forever when there was an interruption. Someone knocked at the front door.

"Who could that be?" said the lady. "Father would use his key, and we never have visitors here."

"I bet you don't!" thought the small spark of Jane, with a last flicker of life.

The lady went to the front door and opened it. A rather small gentleman stood outside. He wore a pointed beard and a nervous expression.

"Good afternoon, madam," he said, putting one hand behind his back as though he were crossing his fingers (which he was). "I am writing a book on child psychology, and I hear you have a very intelligent daughter. I wonder if I might interview her?"

"How interesting!" cried the lady. "I have made a life study of child psychology myself!"

"You have?" said the small gentleman, looking more nervous.

"Yes. What method do you follow, the Schwartz-Metterklume or the Brontossori?"

The small gentleman looked as if he wished he were somewhere else. "I have my own method," he said. "You wouldn't have heard of it."

"But how interesting!" cried the lady. "You must come in and tell me all about it." And she led the small gentleman through the gray hall into the gray drawing room.

Outside, Katharine leaned out from her evergreen hiding place. "Psst," she said.

"Come on," said Mark, from behind his.

And followed by Martha, they crossed the emerald lawn and mounted the front steps of the house. The lady had left the front door ajar in her excitement, and standing in the hallway the children could hear everything that happened in the drawing room perfectly.

"Of course we wouldn't want any publicity," the lady was saying. "You won't use her real name in the book, will you?"

"Naturally not," said the voice of Mr. Smith (for of course the small gentleman was he). "I shall call her chapter The Jane Case."

Mark and Katharine and Martha heard a gasp, as

though the name had meant something to someone in the room.

"Unless of course that is her name?" Mr. Smith's voice went on.

"Oh, no," said the voice of the lady. "We call her Comfort, but her name is Iphigenia."

"If a what?" said Katharine to Mark, in the front doorway.

"Shush," said Mark to Katharine.

"I see," came the voice of Mr. Smith, from the drawing room. "How do you do, Iphigenia? Do you believe in magic?"

"Oh no," came the voice of the lady, before She could answer. "I'm afraid your method is a bit old-fashioned. Iphigenia has never believed in magic, or anything else untrue."

"How sad for her," said the voice of Mr. Smith. "However, what *are* her interests? Does she collect anything, perhaps?"

"Why, yes," said the lady, before She could answer again. "She collects objects of art. Only this afternoon she brought home a rare old talisman!"

In the doorway Martha pinched Katharine. "The charm!" she hissed.

"Shush," Katharine hissed back.

"You don't say?" Mr. Smith's voice sounded excited. "I wonder if I might see if for a moment?"

"I don't see why not," came the voice of the lady. Her footsteps could be heard, crossing the room, and the suspense was more than Mark and Katharine and Martha could bear. They moved across the hall to see what was happening.

The floor of the hall was highly polished and there were some little gray hand-hooked rugs scattered about on it. Martha tripped on one of the rugs, slipped on the floor, and fell into the drawing room with a crash, just as the lady was turning from the curio cabinet with the charm in her hand and Mr. Smith was reaching out his own eager hand to take it. Mark and Katharine followed Martha into the room.

"Hello," said She, smiling at them. After half an hour in the gray house, She liked their looks better than she had at their last meeting. She turned to the gray lady. "These are the children I was playing with this afternoon."

"Well, I'm afraid they are very rude children," said the lady, recovering from her surprise. She looked at Mark and Katharine and Martha sternly. "In this house we don't walk in the front door without being asked. I think you had better go home at once. Iphigenia doesn't want to see you."

"Oh yes, she does, if she only knew it!" said Mark bravely, advancing into the room. "Let me take that charm a minute and I'll prove it. It belongs to us anyway!"

"If you mean this rare old Sanskrit talisman," said the lady, "it certainly does not. It belongs to my Iphigenia."

"She's not yours; she's ours," said Martha, getting up from the floor.

"Her name isn't what you said; it's Jane," said Katharine.

"She doesn't live here; she lives over on Maplewood," said Mark.

"Not another word," said the lady. "Such awful fibbing I never heard! You are either the worst-brought-up children I have ever seen or you are all mentally unbalanced! I'm afraid I shall have to telephone your parents!"

"No, don't do that!" said Mr. Smith, coming forward anxiously. "I'm afraid this is all my fault. I'm afraid I asked these children to come. Just a little experiment, you know. All part of my method."

"Then I don't think much of it," said the lady,

getting really cross. "I don't believe you are a child psychologist at all, or if you are, you shouldn't be allowed to be! I shall write to the *Psychology Journal* and complain!"

"Very well. You're right. I'm not," said Mr. Smith, giving up. "But don't be alarmed; I can explain everything. Only it's a long story; so if you'd just let me have that charm . . ."

"So that's it!" cried the lady. "I see it all now! It's a plot! Coming here pretending to be writing a book, and all the time trying to steal our art treasures! For shame, taking advantage of these unfortunate children!"

"No, no," said Mr. Smith, becoming agitated. "This is all a mistake. That little girl isn't who you think she is at all."

"You wouldn't like her if you got to know her," put in Katharine earnestly. "You would find her a wolf in sheep's clothing."

"She's my sister, only she has what-d'you-call-'ems," said Mark.

"Hallucinations," explained Mr. Smith.

"We want to take her where they'll be kind to her," said Martha. "Jane, Jane, come on home out of this cold, slippery house!"

The remnant of Jane, down in the heart of Iphigenia, heard Martha's call. She thought how much happier she felt with Martha and Mark and Katharine, yes, and Mr. Smith, too, than she did with the gray lady. She remembered her own home and her own family, and wished she belonged to them again. She yearned to answer Martha. And she made a great effort, and forced her way to the surface and started to speak.

But before she could there was an interruption. A thin, gray gentleman appeared in the drawing room.

"Yarworth! Here you are at last!" cried the gray lady. "This criminal, aided by these delinquent children, was trying to rob our Iphigenia!"

"Dear me," said the gray gentleman, retreating slightly. "Are you sure?"

"Don't just stand there!" cried the lady. "Defend us! What will Iphigenia think of her father?"

What Iphigenia would have thought of her father will probably never be known. For at that moment Mr. Smith, having had quite enough of both Iphigenia and her parents, decided to act.

"I'm sorry to appear rude, madam, but you'll be glad of it afterwards," he said. "At least I hope so."

And he snatched the charm from the lady's hand,

took a deep breath, and wished that Jane might be twice as much Jane as she ever was.

Jane, finding herself suddenly herself again, gave a glad cry and ran, much to the surprise of Mark and Katharine and Martha, straight to Mr. Smith.

"You were wonderful," she said. "Part of me was here all along, hoping you'd save me, and you did! You were wonderful!"

"It was nothing," said Mr. Smith, modestly.

"We told you so," said Mark and Katharine to Jane.

They had run to Mr. Smith, too, and so had Martha, and now the five of them stood united, looking defiantly at the gray lady and the gray gentleman.

The lady was blinking her eyes. The gentleman was rubbing his. They looked rather like two people who have just awakened from a nightmare.

"What is the meaning of this intrusion?" demanded the gray lady. "What are you doing in our house? Go away at once!"

"This isn't your little girl, then?" asked Mr. Smith, with his arm around Jane.

The lady looked at Jane with distaste. "I never saw the horrid little thing before in my life!"

"You don't even *have* a little girl, perhaps?" went on Mr. Smith.

"Certainly not," the lady said thankfully. "So noisy and tiresome and such a strain!"

"Then if we take her away with us, it will be quite all right with you?"

"If you don't all leave this house at once, my husband will take steps! Won't you, Yarworth?" said the gray lady.

The gray gentleman took a step backwards in alarm. He did not reply.

"Thank you, madam. That's all I wanted to know," said Mr. Smith. And bowing politely, he touched the charm and made another wish.

Of course if he had asked the four children's advice, they could have told him how to word his second wish much better.

As it was, being new to magic, he didn't put in any of the things experience had taught them, like not being gone too long, and arriving back in a normal way, and their mother's not noticing anything out of the ordinary. He just wished they were twice as far as home again.

And so, a split second later, when the children's mother came into the living room and it was empty, and then suddenly Mr. Smith and the four children were all sitting around it in chairs, she was more than a bit surprised.

"How funny!" she said. "I didn't see you sitting there. I didn't hear a car drive up, either."

She glanced out of the window, and it was then that Mr. Smith remembered that his car was still sitting back on Virginia Street, where he'd parked it, what seemed like ages ago.

He touched the charm in his pocket, and made a quick wish, but not quick enough. When the children's mother looked from the window, first she saw the empty street, then suddenly the car was sitting there.

She put her hand to her head and sat down suddenly.

"I really must go to the doctor about my eyes," she said. "I keep thinking I see the strangest things!"

"It's the sun," said Mr. Smith. "It's awfully strong today."

"*I've* been thinking I saw some awfully strange things this morning, too. Over on Virginia Street," said Mark, daringly, with a wink at Mr. Smith and Jane.

Martha giggled.

"Luncheon is served," said Miss Bick sourly from the doorway, and they all trooped in to where the festive board groaned.

The luncheon party was a great success with the four children, but their mother seemed a bit worried and preoccupied, and kept putting her hand to her forehead as if she were trying to puzzle something out, and this seemed to make Mr. Smith a bit worried, too.

The spirits of the children were so very high, however, that their mother couldn't stay upset for long. And the behavior of Jane, in particular, was enough to warm any mother's faltering heart.

She was so unselfish about second helpings, so eager to pass things without being asked, so tireless in her efforts not to accept the last extra butterscotch tart, lying luscious under its whipped cream, but to bestow it on a friend or relation, so anxious generally to show how much she loved this family above all others, that no one could believe it was the usual good old hasty hot-tempered Jane who sat there among them.

"That charm certainly does improve people, once they've been through the mill of it," Katharine whispered to Mark.

"Whispers at the table shall breakfast in the stable," said their mother.

"Kath was only saying Jane certainly was full of charm this morning," said Mark, with another daring wink at the others.

"Yes, you'd almost think she were a different person!" said Katharine, equally daring.

Martha giggled. So, I regret to say, did Mr. Smith.

"What's the joke?" said the children's mother.

"Oh, nothing," said the four children.

"I'm just feeling happy," said Mr. Smith. "This is a treat for me. I live all alone, you know, and it's years since I've been to a family party like this."

Jane looked round the room, at the colored pictures on the lemon-yellow walls and the gay printed curtains at the window and the bright rugs on the floor and the smiling faces around the table.

"This is a wonderful family to belong to," she said. "It's the best family to belong to in the whole world!"

Then she smiled at Mr. Smith.

"I think *you're* going to think so, too," she said.

7

How It Ended

"Who gets the charm today?" said Martha, early next morning. "We've all had a turn now. Do we start over and take seconds, or should we agree on something and wish it together?"

"I think we ought to give it a day of rest," said Katharine. "After all, today's Sunday."

And once the other children thought about it, they agreed that magic on Sunday didn't seem quite right. Or at least there was a chance that it wouldn't be, and the four children were taking no further chances, now they knew how difficult the charm could be when roused.

So Katharine spent the morning reading *The Ingoldsby Legends,* which she had just discovered, and Mark built derricks with his Meccano set.

Jane humored Martha by playing dolls with her, a pursuit Jane usually scorned, but she was still feeling kindly toward her family, as a result of yesterday's adventure. Her true nature reasserted itself during the course of the game, however, and many a doll was stabbed to the heart or burned at the stake before the morning was over.

The four children all hated big noon dinners on Sunday; so when hunger reared its hideous head they just had soup and toast, and it was right after that that Mr. Smith arrived, and asked if they and their mother wouldn't like to come for a drive with him, and a picnic supper afterwards. He said he knew of a wonderful picnic place with a river and swings and a meadow and woods, and he had had six box lunches made up at Meinert's Pastry Shop.

Jane and Mark and Katharine and Martha could hardly wait to start.

"What is it that makes box lunches always sound so delicious?" Katharine wondered. "It makes you think there might be almost anything inside. Duck eggs and nectar and kinds of sandwiches nobody ever had before!"

Their mother said she had a headache and thought she'd better stay home, which didn't sound like her at all. The four children stared at her.

"You never have headaches," said Mark.

"You never want to stay home and spoil things, either," said Katharine.

"It won't be any fun without you," said Jane.

And of course after that the children's mother had to give in, and five minutes later away they went.

The picnic place proved to be all that was ideal, as Mr. Smith had said it would. Martha went picking butterfly weed in the meadow, only it seemed to be beeweed, too, and one stung her, and Katharine wandered romantically through the woods, and was almost sure she saw a snake, and Jane and Mark tried to build stepping stones across the river and fell in with all their clothes on, and altogether it was a typical happy family outing.

The box lunches turned out not to contain any duck eggs or nectar, but the sandwiches were sufficiently unusual, and there were deviled eggs and potato salad and lots of little assorted cakes that the children had fun with, deciding which ones they liked best and trying to trade off the others.

Supper was eaten round a bonfire deftly constructed by Mark and Mr. Smith, and stories were told and songs were sung, until what with one thing and another, it was long after nine o'clock when they packed themselves into the car once more, and drove home through the purple darkness.

And the four children were all so tired and happy and sunburned and sleepy that they went straight to bed with almost no ado.

Martha, as sometimes happens, was so tired that she couldn't seem to go to sleep, and she noticed that Mr. Smith didn't go home right away, but sat talking to their mother for what seemed like hours and hours.

And much later, in the middle of the night, she woke up, possibly as a result of too many cakes, and was almost sure she heard their mother crying.

This couldn't be, of course. Martha had never heard of a mother who cried, and certainly not *their* mother, so happy and strong and busy and sensible, and the pride of the Toledo *News-Bee!*

She tiptoed to the door and listened, but there didn't seem to be any sound now. She decided with relief that she must have been mistaken, and went back to bed and to sleep.

But in the morning their mother hardly said a word at breakfast, and her cheeks looked pale and her eyes looked tired, and Martha began to wonder again.

After breakfast, when their mother had gone to work, Jane, whose new family devotion continued to shine forth, volunteered to do the dishes alone and unaided, and this brilliant example so bestirred the finer feelings of Mark and Katharine that they insisted on helping.

Martha followed them out into the kitchen, and sat watching, and wondering whether her worries about their mother were too farfetched for her to mention them.

"Does everyone realize we've had the charm a week now?" Jane was saying, scraping toast crumbs off plates and then plunging the plates in soapy water.

"Really?" said Katharine. "It seems like months, at least."

Mark began counting it out. "The fire was Tuesday and the desert was Wednesday, we met Launcelot on Thursday and went to the movies on Friday, Jane belonged to that other family on Saturday, and we rested on Sunday."

"And today's Monday," said Jane. "The seventh day. I read somewhere that seven's a magic number. Maybe today'll be the biggest wish yet."

"When you come to think of it, no great big lasting thing has happened so far," said Mark. "We've had lots of adventures, but we're still just the same as we were before we found it."

"Our characters are improved," said Katharine, "and I think we're sort of happier."

"I don't think Mother is," said Martha.

Three faces turned to her, and, "What do you mean?" said three voices at once.

But before Martha could answer, the telephone in the hall began to ring.

Mark got there first.

"Hello?" he said. "Oh, hi." He turned to the others. "It's Mr. Smith."

"Let me," said Jane, grabbing the phone.

"Honestly," Mark complained to Katharine. "After we had all that hard work getting her to like him at all, now you'd think he were her own special property!"

"Yes," Jane was saying into the phone excitedly. "Yes. All right. We will. Yes, right away!"

She hung up, and turned from the phone, looking serious and important. "Big Council meeting! At the bookshop in twenty minutes. Carfare will be refunded. Can we scrape together the wherewithal?"

The week had been given over so completely to magic experiment that allowances remained practically intact; so that was all right.

"Are we taking the charm?" Martha wanted to know.

"Naturally! What else would an Important Council be about?" said Jane, witheringly.

Katharine fetched the charm from its hiding place, and the four children waited for a moment when Miss Bick's attention was elsewhere (elsewhere being with the gas-meter man) to steal down the front stairs, hurry out the door, and run two blocks up Bancroft Street before waiting for the streetcar, so she wouldn't see them from the window and take unpleasant steps.

The ride downtown seemed endless but turned

out at last not to be, and ten minutes later found them hurrying into the bookshop.

Mr. Smith rose from his desk, and came to greet them. He seemed uneasy.

"Hello," he said. "You were quicker than I expected. Please sit down. I have something to tell you."

The four children looked around, but there were piles of books on all the sitting places; so they stayed standing. Mr. Smith didn't seem to notice. He hesitated, cleared his throat, took his handkerchief out and put it away again, and looked at the floor.

"Dear me, I find this very difficult," he said. "I think perhaps first of all it might help if you stopped calling me Mr. Smith and called me Hugo."

Jane shuddered. "I *couldn't!*"

"That's a terrible name," said Mark, ever candid.

"Maybe if we shortened it?" Katharine suggested. "Hugh isn't so bad."

"I shall call him Huge," announced Martha independently. "After all, he looms huge in our future, if you-know-what is going to happen! You know, if he's going to be our—" she broke off, and uttered the last word in a piercing whisper that carried to all corners of the room—"*stepfather!*"

Mr. Smith heard the whisper, and a blush mantled his cheek.

"Then you know!" he said. "And here I was wondering how to break it to you. That's what I had to tell you. It's true. I have come to care very deeply for your mother and have asked her to be my wife."

"We thought you would," said Martha.

"Any day now," said Mark.

"We think it's wonderful," said Katharine.

"Specially me," said Jane.

"Thank you," said Mr. Smith. "You are four very pleasant children, and I should be proud and happy to be your stepfather, and you may call me Huge or anything else you like."

"*Uncle* Huge," said Mark. "It's more respectful."

"There is only one difficulty," said Mr. Smith.

"Won't she have you?" asked Katharine. "Is she being coy and hard to please?"

"I could go and reason with her if you like," offered Mark. "I'm quite good at it, really."

"*I* shall tell her I think she's a very lucky woman to have landed you!" said Martha.

"Please, I beg of you, do not say anything of the kind!" cried Mr. Smith in alarm, blushing again. "No. Your mother has admitted that she thinks she could care for me in return. But yesterday evening she told me definitely that her answer is no. The reason is that she believes herself to be ill. Mentally ill. I leave you to guess why."

"She's noticed things," said Jane. "Us appearing suddenly out of nowhere and things."

"That wish she half got, when she ran into you out on Bancroft Street," said Katharine.

"Me with all those diamonds and robbers," said Mark.

"I *did* hear her crying last night, then," said Martha.

"Oh, dear. Was she?" said Mr. Smith.

"That's bad," said Mark.

"And it's all our fault," said Katharine.

The four children looked solemn. Then Jane's face cleared.

"It's all right. We can fix it up," she said. "What could be simpler? We'll confess. We'll tell her the whole thing from the beginning."

"Do you think she'll believe it?" said Mr. Smith. "Remember, your mother is a very practical person."

"Stubborn, too," agreed Katharine.

"We could *show* her," suggested Mark doubtfully. "We could have the charm take her somewhere."

"That's it!" Jane's eyes were shining. "We'll let her wish—we'll give her whatever her heart desires! This will be the best deed yet! Come on, let's go over there right now!"

"Do be careful," said Mr. Smith. "Hadn't we better plan it out, first?"

But his words were wasted on the bookshop air. Jane had the charm in her hand, and rashly, excitedly, without thinking what she'd do when they got there, she wished.

The next moment they were in their mother's office.

The children's mother was Women's Club Editor of the newspaper, and that meant that she wrote all those little pieces that say which ladies are going to meetings at which other ladies' houses and what they are going to have to eat.

It wasn't a very important job, and her office was tiny, and today it was already quite filled by a fat lady who was telling their mother all about the Potluck Pageant she was planning to give for the League of Needless Women.

So that when Jane and Mark and Katharine and Martha and Mr. Smith were suddenly all there in the office, too, it made quite a crowd.

"Oh!" cried their mother, turning pale, as the five familiar figures appeared out of nowhere before her gaze. "There it is, happening again!"

"Really!" said the fat lady to Jane and Katharine and Martha, who were wedged tightly against her. "Stop shoving."

"I'm sorry, but we haven't time for you now," said Jane to the fat lady. And she wished her twice as far as where she belonged.

The lady was quite annoyed to find herself suddenly at home in her own kitchen, and later sued the newspaper for witchcraft. But she was never able to prove her case, and anyway that does not come into this story.

Back in her office, the children's mother sat staring palely at the place where the lady had been.

"It's all right," Jane told her. "We know what you're thinking, but you're wrong. We can explain everything."

"What you thought was you going crazy was just us," said Martha.

"We've got a magic charm," said Mark.

"We've had it for a week, only we didn't tell you," said Katharine. "We thought you were too old to know."

"And that night you went to see Aunt Grace and Uncle Edwin and wished you were home, *you* had it," said Jane. "And it works by halves. And that's how you happened to meet Mr. Smith. And that proves what a good charm it is, because we think he'd make a wonderful stepfather and not a bit Murdstone, and we've adopted him for our Uncle Huge, and we think you ought to marry him right away!"

Their mother looked at Mr. Smith reproachfully.

"You told them!" she said. "And now they're making all this up to make me feel better. How could you?"

"No, that isn't it at all," said Jane. "There really *is* a charm! Look." And she put the charm in their mother's hands.

"That's a nickel," said their mother.

"That's what I thought at first, too," said Jane, "but it isn't. See, it's got old ancient signs on it! Wish, why don't you? That'll prove it. For whatever your heart desires! Or wait, I'll show you how." And she touched the charm, where it lay in their mother's hand.

"I wish," she began, trying to think of something simple and harmless, yet unusual. "I wish two birds would fly in the window and speak to us."

Immediately a chickadee flew in through the window and stood on the desk.

"Hello," it said. It flew out again.

Their mother had her eyes shut tight. "Tell it to go away!" she said.

"It just did," said Martha.

Their mother opened her eyes again. "That proves it," she said. "It's just as I was afraid it was! Everything's been too much for me and my mind's given way."

"Now, now," said Mr. Smith. "You mustn't get excited." But Mark interrupted him.

"Honestly!" he said to Jane in disgust. "Making birds come in and talk to her! No wonder she thinks she's crazy! Whose heart's desire would that be? No, don't you remember how she always used to say she wanted to be City Editor of the paper some day? Let me have that." And he took the charm from Jane.

"Careful!" said Mr. Smith.

"It's all right. I know what to say," Mark reassured him. And he wished.

The owner of the newspaper walked into the office.

"Ah, dear lady," he said. "How happy you look with your little family around you!"

Their mother turned a woebegone face upon him and said nothing.

"What part of Mother's little family is Mr. Smith?" whispered Katharine to Mark, giggling.

"Shush," said Mark.

"We are making some changes in the organization," the owner of the paper went on, "and I am glad to tell you that from this moment on you may consider yourself City Editor, at a sizeable increase in salary."

"No," said the children's mother, shaking her head stubbornly. "It isn't true. It's just some horrible crazy dream! You aren't even real. You're just a . . . a figment of my imagination!"

"Well, really!" said the owner of the paper, looking displeased. Apparently he did not like being called a figment.

"Aw, Mother," said Mark. "Don't worry; just take it. Don't you remember how you've always said you could run the paper singlehanded better than the rest of this whole dopey crowd down here does?"

"You don't say!" said the owner of the paper, coldly. "In that case, perhaps I had better withdraw my offer. Perhaps you had better look for a job somewhere else!" And he made a dignified exit.

"This is worse and worse!" moaned the children's mother. "Now I'm unemployed! And he'll tell everybody it's because I've gone raving, tearing mad, and he'll be right, because I *have!*"

"There, there," Katharine soothed her. "Mark just didn't know. He couldn't, because I'm the only one who knows what your heart's desire really is!" She turned to the others. "Mother told me once that when she was our age she always wanted to be a bareback rider." And Katharine took the charm in her hand.

"Dear me, I hardly think—" began Mr. Smith.

But before he could finish his sentence Katharine had wished, and he and the four children found themselves sitting in the front row of the grandstand inside an immense circus tent, and the ringmaster was just cracking his whip and announcing that La Gloria, the Best Bareback Rider in the World, would now perform her death-defying act.

There was a crash of cymbals, and La Gloria rode into the ring on a white horse. La Gloria was the children's mother. Only she didn't look at all like herself in pink tights and a frilly skirt. And she didn't act like herself, either.

She rode round the ring with grace and speed,

and jumped her horse through hoops with spirit and style. And, what was most alarming of all to the four children, she seemed to be *enjoying* it!

"Hoop-la!" she cried. "Allez-oop! Whee!"

"Stop her!" wailed Martha. "She'll hurt herself! She'll fall!" And she jumped over the rail and ran into the middle of the ring, with Jane and Mark and Mr. Smith behind her. Forgetting the charm in her hand, Katharine ran with them. La Gloria had to rein in her horse to keep from running them down.

"Get out of the way! You're spoiling the act!" she said haughtily.

"This is awful! She doesn't know us!" cried Martha.

"Of course she does. Don't you?" said Jane.

"No, and I don't wish to!" said La Gloria. "Out of the way! The show must go on!"

"Why?" said Mark, ever willing to argue a point.

Behind them in the grandstand the audience was beginning to be restless.

"In my opinion people who interrupt other peopie's entertainment should be ejected!" said a lady in the front row.

"You're right!" said the lady sitting next to her. "They should be ejected first and then put out!"

An angry murmur began to grow.

"Down in front!" yelled somebody.

"Get the hook!" yelled somebody else.

The ringmaster approached, cracking his whip.

Then, just as it looked as though there might be unpleasantness, Katharine unwished, and they found themselves back in the newspaper office.

Their mother sat at her desk, a dreamy, faraway smile on her face. Katharine turned to her anxiously.

"There!" she said. "*Now* do you believe?"

Their mother's smile vanished. She looked stubborn. "That didn't happen," she said. "It was a dream."

"How do we all know about it, then?" said Katharine.

"You don't," said their mother. "You couldn't." And nothing any of the children could say would make her believe anything else. After five minutes of trying, they were all breathing hard and beginning to feel a bit desperate.

"May I point out," said Mr. Smith, at last, "that if you would only listen to me —"

But Martha interrupted him.

"Of course if you ask *me,*" she said, "the trouble is, none of those wishes were any good because we didn't make her *believe* first."

The others looked at her.

"Of course," said Mark.

"Out of the mouths of babes," said Jane.

"Why didn't *we* think of that?" said Katharine. "Naturally you have to believe in magic — otherwise if it starts happening to you all sanity is despaired of!"

"Exactly," said Mr. Smith. "Now I suggest —"

But Martha had the charm in her hand.

"Oh, Mother," she said earnestly. "Mother *dear,* if you just wouldn't be so stubborn about it! I *wish* you'd believe what we keep telling you! I wish it twice!"

"I do, dear. I believe you," said their mother.

"You believe there's a magic charm?"

"Naturally, dear. If you say so, dear."

"And everything's all right and you're going to get married and live happily ever after?"

"Whatever you say, dear."

"There!" Martha turned in triumph to the others.

But Mark was looking at their mother suspiciously.

"Something's wrong here," he said. "That doesn't sound like Mother at all!"

"No, it doesn't, does it, dear?" said their mother.

"We don't want a mother that just *agrees* with everything all the time!"

"No, you don't, do you, dear?" said their mother. "I wouldn't either."

"You see what I mean?" said Mark. "Why, I bet if I said the *moon* was made of green cheese she'd just say, 'Yes, dear. I know, dear.'"

"Isn't it true?" said their mother. "I couldn't agree with you more, dear."

The other three were just as alarmed as Mark by now.

"This is awful!" Jane cried, turning on Martha. "You've taken Mother and turned her into some awful sappy blah character without any gumption at all! Why, Mr. Smith won't even want to marry her in this condition!"

"No, he won't, will he?" said their mother, contentedly. "I wouldn't, either."

There was a stunned silence.

"And *now,*" said Mr. Smith, in a grim voice, "perhaps you will permit me to make a suggestion?"

No one had the heart to reply.

Mr. Smith took the charm from Martha's hand firmly.

"I suggest that we start over," he said, "and I suggest that we take it more slowly. And that *somebody* thinks before acting!" And he held the charm out before him solemnly, almost as if he were in church.

"I wish first that Alison may be restored to her own natural, stubborn, lovable self, and I wish this twice. But I further wish that her mind, without losing any of its natural, stubborn, lovable character, may be made open to receiving the secret of this charm, and this I also wish twice. And I thirdly wish that she may be twice relieved of the fear that has come to her through the magic of this charm, and may be twice ready to receive any boon it may grant her."

There was another silence. Then the children's mother looked round at them all, and smiled. And it was plain that these last wild minutes, ever since they had arrived in the office, had vanished from her mind.

"Hello," she said. "How nice of you all to come and surprise me."

"We came," said Mr. Smith, "to bring you a gift." And he put the charm on her desk. "This is a magic charm, and it works by halves. Ask twice for whatever you wish, and you will receive it once. It is from all of us, with our love. Now. What is your heart's desire?"

"But you know what it is," said the children's mother, not picking up the charm. "My heart's desire is to marry you and have the children love you as much as I do. And not to have to work on the paper anymore, but stay home and take care of the children instead of having to have Miss Bick. And to have the children be able to go to the country in the summers the way they've always wanted to. And to have you shave off that beard."

"Really? Don't you like it?" said Mr. Smith, in surprise. "I've grown rather attached to it, through the years. I'll hate to see it go. But for the rest of your desire, if you marry me I'll do my best to give it to you. Without the help of any charm. We won't be rich, because people who run bookshops seldom are, but summers in the country I think I can manage."

He took their mother's hand, and the two of them stood looking at each other.

"Aren't you going to wish?" said Katharine, after a bit.

"Why should we?" said their mother. "We *have* our happiness."

"Oh," said Katharine, disappointed.

The faces of the four children fell. They had never felt so let-down in all their lives. Then after a moment Katharine's face brightened.

"But it was a wish that brought you together in the first place," she said, "and it was another wish that made you meet again. It was really the charm that caused everything, in a way!"

"Maybe that's the one big, important thing it came into our lives to do," said Mark.

"You mean maybe now it's used up and won't work anymore?" said Martha, alarmed.

"Oh, and today's the seventh day, too!" cried Jane. "Maybe the magic's over!" She picked up the charm and turned to Mr. Smith. "I don't want to butt in, and I'm sure you could give Mother her heart's desire by the sweat of your manly brow alone," she said, "but just to make sure, I wish all her wishes would come true twice!"

Mr. Smith gave a cry, and clapped his hand to the place where his beard used to be. The four children agreed later that he looked very handsome without it.

Only right now they didn't notice, because right now other things were happening.

For it seemed as though the room suddenly began to shine, and there seemed to be a sound of far-off singing and a faint chiming of bells all about them. And a fragrance hung in the air that was not quite cinnamon and not quite vanilla and not quite the perfume of all the gardens in the world, but a little like all these things and something else, too. It was the scent of magic.

And their mother and Mr. Smith stood looking at each other and didn't see the shining or hear the singing or sense the fragrance because all they saw was the light of each other's eyes, and all they heard was the beating of each other's heart and all they felt was their love for each other.

By and by the shining and the singing and the fragrance died away.

"I guess that's the last wish, all right," said Mark. "It never rang bells and smelled like a perfume shop before!"

"What did you say?" said their mother.

"I said I guess that's the last wish," said Mark. "The last wish on the charm."

"What charm?" said Mr. Smith.

They had forgotten. Now that they had their heart's desire, they had no need of any other magic. They turned and went out of the office, and the four children followed them.

Jane still held the charm in her hand, but the children were as sure as they had ever been of anything in their short, full lives that with that last wish the magic had gone out of it, and that there would be no more enchanted adventures for them.

"Still," said Mark, as they reached the street, and just as though the others had spoken their thoughts aloud. "Still, we might as well test it and see. Wish something. Any old dumb thing."

"All right, I wish I had four noses," said Jane.

Everyone looked. But the usual slightly snub one remained the only feature in the middle of the face of Jane.

"That settles that," said Mark. "Good-bye, charm." But his voice was quite cheerful.

"I guess it just came to make us happy," said Katharine. "And now we are!"

"Weren't we happy before?" asked Martha.

"Oh, sure, in a kind of way," said Mark. "The way some people are happy and some people are unhappy because they're born that way. But there were a lot of things we wanted changed, and now they're going to be!"

"No more Miss Bick!" said Katharine.

"Summers in the country," said Jane, "and a practically perfect stepfather! You know," she added, feeling suddenly rather wonderful, "it looks as if *we* got our heart's desire, too!"

But all the same, she didn't throw the old, used-up charm away. As they hurried to catch up with their mother and Mr. Smith, she stopped long enough to put it away carefully in her handbag.

She would keep it a while longer, just in case.

8

How It Began Again

And it turned out there was one more wish, after all.

The last wish was Jane's alone, and she never really knew she made it.

That night, as she was getting undressed, she found the charm in her pocket, and sat on the bed looking at it for a long time, and pondering the mystery of how it had come into their hands, and why.

And from that she went on to thinking about their mother's being married, and the changes it would bring into their lives.

She was quite contented about everything. But because she was the only one of the four children who remembered their father, she would have been more contented still if she could have felt sure that he knew about what was going to happen, and approved of it.

It had been a full day, and she was ready for sleep. Already her eyes had begun to close of their own accord. But as she put out the light and tucked the charm absentmindedly under her pillow, her last waking thought was that she wished her father were with her now, so she'd know how he felt about things.

She wasn't worrying about the charm, or working out the right fractions, as she wished it. But because there was still this one small corner in Jane that wasn't completely happy, the charm relented, and thawed out of its icy used-upness, and granted the wish, according to its well-known fashion. Immediately her father was *half* there.

He was there like a thought in her mind, assuring her that everything was all right, and exactly as he would want it, and that he was happy in their happiness.

And a wonderful feeling of peace filled the heart of Jane, and she went to sleep with a smile on her face.

In the morning she'd forgotten all about the wish. She knew only that the sun was yellow and warm, and the sky was blue, and a golden future lay ahead, and all was right with the world.

She found the charm under her pillow when she was making her bed, and put it in the top bureau drawer, reminding herself to consult with the others later about what to do with it.

But the next days were so full, what with plans for the wedding, that Jane never did get around to consulting.

And at last the wedding day came, and happy was the bride the sun shone on, and happy, too, were the four children. And after their mother and Mr. Smith had been pronounced man and wife, Mr. Smith shook hands all round, and their mother kissed them, and then off the two of them went for a week's honeymoon, and Miss Bick came and stayed with the children for the last time, and had her will with them for seven days, and biffed and banged and cleaned and complained until life became a mere burden, but there was always the comforting thought that at the end of the seven days lay freedom.

And the seven days finally were over, and their mother and Mr. Smith returned, and the four children sang "Good-bye forever!" out of the upstairs windows as Miss Bick took her departure for the last time.

And it was then that their mother told them that Mr. Smith had taken a house on a lake for the rest of the summer, where it was real country all around, and yet it was near enough for him to drive in to the bookshop every day.

So from then on all was bustle and squeak, in the words of Katharine, and if the children weren't being taken downtown to buy bathing suits and camera film and badminton birds and beach balls, they were walking to the library and choosing vacation reading or packing their nice shabby old suitcases and the nicer new ones Mr. Smith had bought them.

And it wasn't until the morning of the day before they were to leave that Jane got around to cleaning out her top bureau drawer, and found the charm again.

Immediately she summoned a Council.

"Do you suppose we ought to keep it forever, sort of In Memoriam?" she wondered.

"Put it in the curio cabinet with the other objects of art," said Katharine, giggling.

"Maybe we ought to try it again," said Martha. "Maybe it was just tired before, and now it's had a nice rest!"

"Huh-uh." Mark shook his head. "That last wish was the end. You could tell."

And the others had to agree that you could. But Martha still wasn't pacified.

"What about this, then?" she said. "It's used up for us, but how do we know it wouldn't still be perfectly good for other people?"

This was a thrilling idea.

"Sure," said Mark. "It stands to reason. It's come down through centuries with its magic un-scathed—it'd take more than four paltry children to make it bite the dust!"

Jane nodded excitedly. "You mean now we pass it on to somebody else!"

"Anybody we know?" Katharine wondered.

"We could go round being sort of fairy godmothers and granting wishes," said Martha.

Mark shook his head.

"That's no good. We'd just get so we wanted to tell everybody what to wish. It'd be sort of like trying to have the charm all over again, secondhand. I think that would be kind of against the rules. It came to us out of the unknown, and I think that's where it ought to go again. I think we ought to let some utter stranger find it, and then put it out of our minds forever."

And the others had to agree that this *did* seem like the kind of noble conduct the charm would expect of them.

So it was with feelings of crusader-like righteousness that, five minutes later, the four children got off a streetcar in a part of town they didn't know at all, and stood looking around them.

Lots of people walked past, but they were all grown-ups.

"And I think it has to be a child," said Mark. "Most grown-ups wouldn't understand, unless they're wonderful ones like Mr. Smith, and you don't find types like him on every street corner."

At last they saw a little girl heading their way. The little girl had a baby with her. The baby was very young and fat, and just learning to walk, and was exceedingly slow about it. As the little girl came nearer,

the four children could see that her face, while pleasant, was tired and pale.

"She looks as if she could do with some happiness," said Katharine.

The others nodded.

So Jane dropped the charm on the sidewalk, in a
place where it would glint in the sun and attract attention, and she and Mark and Katharine and Martha
hid behind a rather scraggly privet hedge nearby, and
waited.

"Oh, come along, Baby. Hurry up!" they heard
the little girl saying. But Baby wouldn't be hurried.
It walked even slower, putting each foot down carefully and then looking at it to be sure that it landed
on solid ground. And the third time it looked down
it saw the glint of the charm.

Before the horrified gaze of the four children, the
baby picked the charm up clumsily, and looked at
it. Then the worst happened. It put the charm in its
mouth and swallowed.

Behind the hedge everyone gasped.

"Is it lost forever, do you think, or will it come up
again?" asked Martha.

"It's a long red lane that has no turning," remarked
Katharine.

"Now I suppose the *baby'll* get a wish," said Martha. "What do you suppose it'll be?"

"Probably something horrible," said Jane, "and nobody'll know or be able to help it because it can't talk and tell them!"

"Don't worry," said Mark. "It'll probably just be about Pablum or something."

And it wasn't the baby who got the wish, after all. For now the weary little girl, growing tired of walking so slowly, picked the baby up and began to carry it.

"Oh dear, Baby," she said. "I wish you didn't weigh so much. I wish you didn't weigh anything at all."

And because she was holding the baby who held the charm, right away the magic began to begin again.

Of course if she'd got her wish whole, the baby would have left the earth and gone shooting off into space. As it was, the charm did its usual trick, and immediately the baby weighed half as little as nothing at all, which is still very little. It left the girl's arms, bounced up toward the sky, then floated gently earthward like a piece of thistledown.

The little girl caught it, but it went bouncing up again. The little girl began to cry.

"Shall we tell her?" said Katharine.

"Wait," said Mark.

They waited. And the bouncing did its work. The third time the little girl caught the baby, something shiny flew out of its mouth and landed clinking on the sidewalk. The little girl saw the shine and heard the clink. She put the baby down, and ran to pick up the charm.

She stood looking at it. Then she looked back at the baby, who had ceased to bounce and was sitting on the sidewalk with its thumb in its mouth.

And then, plain as day, the four children could see the little girl beginning to think, and to put two and two together. A look of wild wonder and excitement came over her face, the look of one who is about to make a magic wish.

And it was then that Mark, ever strong-minded, dragged the others away.

"Oughtn't we to tell her the secret?" said Jane. "About saying two times everything?"

"Nobody told us, did they?" said Mark. "I don't think anyone's supposed to."

He wouldn't even let the others look back as they boarded the street car.

"You never know — we might be turned into pillars of salt or something," he said. "I don't think we're supposed to know anything about it. Something tells me."

"At least we know she'll be happy in the end," said Katharine.

But Martha couldn't help wanting to know what was happening right now. When Mark wasn't watching her, she turned and looked.

The little girl and the baby had vanished, on what wild errand of adventure Martha could only guess. But she would never know. She would be left to wonder all the rest of her life.

And she wondered something else, too. After they'd ridden a few blocks, she put it into words.

"Do you suppose we'll ever have any more magic adventures?" she said. "Oh, maybe not big ones like these, but any at all? Just nice little safe ones, maybe?"

"I wonder," said Jane.

Mark and Katharine didn't say anything, but they were wondering, too.

But it was a long time before the four children knew the answer.